For My *Savage,*
I Will *Ride* or *Die*

Killany & Yung's Story

By:

Nikki Nicole

Acknowledgements

Hey, guys, this is my third book. I was so excited to do this book. I was in a great writing space when I wrote this book. I want to thank Shan for giving me the opportunity to showcase my talent and skills. I was bugging her about my book. She knows it too; from emails to social media. I appreciate all of my readers from the Baby I Play for Keeps series. I appreciate all the feedback that you gave me. I researched it, figured out what to do, and it was on from there. I also wanted to thank my publisher, Monique McGraw Pearson. Boss Lady, you are the best, It's a pleasure working with you; we clicked instantly. I'm glad that you were willing to take a chance on me! I got your back forever. Grand Penz Publications we are on the way, I promise you that.

I would like to thank God, first and foremost for the gift and talent; without Him, there would be no me. I would like to thank my husband, Mr. Taylor for keeping me motivated to do this. Shout out to my kids: De 'Mauri, Kelsea, Kiara, Shelby, and Mariyah. When I started writing this series, my kids were so interested they started writing a book. I want to give a shout out to my mom also; she told me to push this pen because I have a story to tell! Last but not least, I have to give a shout out to my squad; Sonya Hardimon, if it weren't for you, I wouldn't have started reading books. You turned me on to Urban Fiction a year ago, now, I'm writing Urban Fiction. You stay in my ear telling me what to do and how to do it, and you make sure I'm bringing it every chapter. I got you forever and a day!!

Shout out to my beta readers; Barbie White, Wahketta Davis, Latonya Davis, Rashida Morris, and Antwonia Mack, I appreciate you guys. I stay screaming, "ain't no chicks like the ones I got." You guys kept me motivated to do this series. Y'all liked it and kept it real every time about what I needed to do and what I needed to change.

I'd like to give a shout out to the funniest readers that I've met these past few months; Valentina Foster, Ella Shannon, Ava Royal, Padrica Kennedy, and

Snowie Moffett. I loved your reviews and the fuel you guys gave me the energy to keep pushing.

To my new readers, you can check out Baby I Play for Keeps 1&2 by yours truly, Nikki Nicole available now on Amazon. Please leave a review, authors love that, good or bad.

Follow me on Facebook at Nikki favored Nicole

Join My Reading Group: Dope Urban Reads

Email me: authoressnikkinicole@gmail.com

Good Reads Authoress Nikki Nicole

Check Out These Awesome Books Also

The Power of Our Love Series by Quanna Lashae

Imani Series by Ashley Robinson

She's My Forever, He's My Eternity by Ashley Robinson

Chapter 1

Menya

Armony and I were flying to New Orleans to meet KC, Cartier, and Yung for the weekend. KC insisted that I needed to stay at home because Cartier wasn't fucking with me like that anymore. The only logical reason that I could think of that he would say that is because Cartier had to have brought somebody down there with him. That has nothing to do with me. Shit, if it goes sideways, me and Armony will wreck with whoever. It's nothing. We do this shit for fun. I feel sorry for whoever it is because their weekend was about to be hell fucking with us.

"Cartier doesn't want me to come, huh?" I asked "Let me guess he has some bitch down there with him. Oh well, he knew what it was, and we knew what it is, too."

He and his bitch will feel me too, watch. Let me introduce myself, my name is Menya Olawoyue. I'm Armony's best friend. Cartier and I have been dating on and off for about a year. I'm five-foot-four, one hundred thirty-six pounds of pure chocolate, with dimples, a fat ass, no waist, banging shape, and pouty lips. My hair is jet black, fuck that natural shit. I didn't understand why everybody was going natural anyway. I had a good ass super perm with extra strength, but my shit was nice. Enough about me, I can't wait to cut up and ruin Cartier's and his bitch's little trip.

"Yes bitch, he doesn't want you to come. That has to be the reason. I know you're going to be on your best behavior, *not!* Let's get to the airport now. I'm anxious to see who's with him. I'm packed and ready to go," Armony laughed. *Let the games begin. KC is about to be pissed with me. Oh well.*

"You better not be friends with that bitch either," She laughed. Armony was so desperate, her dumb ass will try to be friends with anybody, just watch. I really wanted KC, he was paid. I don't know what Armony did to get him, but it worked, he wasn't budging.

"I told you not to fuck with him, but no, you insisted on fucking with him. You don' fucked around and caught feelings, and now he ain't fucking with you. You should know better," Armony I assured her. *I told her ass, but she went behind my back fucking with him. Now she's looking stupid.*

Killany

Yung and I were on our way to New Orleans. It was actually pretty cool to be in his presence. I haven't kicked it with a guy that I was feeling in a very long time. I wouldn't say that I was picky. I just haven't met anybody that piqued my interest. I was a little curious about him. His whole persona and demeanor spoke volumes. He commanded attention. It's a lot of frauds out here, so I was going to move with caution. I hated that he refused to let me pack a bag, but I needed to get a few items from my sister's house. I had my favorite bitch with me, my Desert Eagle. I call her Shelly. She leaves shell casings everywhere; she'll never leave me lonely.

"Talk to me, Killany. Can I call you Kill? We have a six-hour drive ahead of us, the silent treatment won't work. Tell me about yourself. I like your voice. I like the way you talk, too, I could listen to you talk all day," Yung blurted. *She knows she's not quiet, Shorty was too lit earlier.*

"No, you can't call me Kill. You know enough about me, tell me about you. I'm sure my mom gave you the rundown, that's why I'm skeptical on what to say because it's no telling what she could've told you," I laughed. *My mom was extra, I loved her dearly.*

"Your mom is wild, man. She didn't say much. She said some things, but I'll have to figure out if they're true or not. I want to know more about you from you, and nobody else," Yung blurted out. *Here she goes with that talking in circles shit, her mom did mention that.*

"I'm twenty-five, my birthday is next Friday, and I'm a twin. I'm a daddy's girl, I'm single, I live in Virginia, and I stay to myself," She answered. "Is that enough for you? Tell me about you." *I want to know what makes him interested in getting to know me.*

"I don't do much talking. I believe in showing you the real me. I could talk all day about how real I am and what I could do for you, I'd rather show you," Yung retorted. *I don't like to brag, I'm a man of very few words.*

***

When we finally made it to New Orleans, it was after two AM. I could actually see Yung and I kicking it. He was pretty cool. We talked and laughed the whole ride. I drove for three hours so he could get some rest, but he watched me the whole time. I told him to rest his eyes. I could tell Yung was heavy in the streets, and didn't sleep much. If he'd let me, I could change that. Raven had shot me a text earlier and said she would see me tomorrow, she was riding out with Cartier. We pulled up to our hotel, the Hilton Garden Inn located in the French Quarter. I woke Yung up so we could valet park. We checked in and made our way to our room. We had a very nice suite. I needed to shower and handle my hygiene. I made sure the shower was extra hot. I was tired too and ready to lay it down. I already knew as soon as I hit the sheets, it was a wrap. I noticed there was only one bed. I knew I was going to enjoy this trip lying next to Yung and tucked in his arms. Let me get my mind out the gutter.

"Damn Ma, did I miss something? It's two AM, and you're blushing in the shower. What has your attention? Let me join you?" Yung smiled. She made her way to the shower quick. I was getting in with her whether she liked it or not. I needed a hot shower too. I was anxious to see what she looked like naked.

"Sure, you can join me, I'm almost finished, though, no touching," I laughed.

Damn, Yung was hung like a horse. He had a big ass dick. My nipples were hard, and my pussy was tingling. He's the biggest I've seen thus far.

"No touching huh?" Yung asked. Damn she was sexy, I didn't even know she was tatted, her back was covered with roses and vines, and she had two hearts on her ass. I wanted to bend her over and fuck her right where she stood, I'm patient, though. She tried to ease up out of the shower, but I pulled her body into mine.

"I told you no touching, right? You're a really bad boy. I have to teach you like a child huh," I promised. The way Yung grabbed me up in the shower and pulled my body next to his, I knew this is the only place that I'd rather be. It felt so right, I started to spread my legs open for easy access.

"You don't have to teach me shit, I break all the rules no matter the circumstances. Keep fucking with me, and you'll see," Yung assured her. He pushed me out the shower and smacked me on my ass, I'm not with that teasing shit.

I dried off and put lotion on my body. *I see now Yung is going to break me out of my celibacy. He has dick swinging everywhere. That big motherfucker damn near touches his knees. I didn't even bring a bag, so you know*

I'm sleeping nude. This is a slick motherfucker. Oh well, it is what it is. We're both grown. If it happens, it happens. This bed is calling my name I wouldn't mind messing up the covers and shit, Killany she thought to herself.

"I had to jack off, and I normally don't do that shit. Killany is doing something to me that I don't like. I'm a rude ass nigga. If I want anything, I get it, and that pussy that's in between her legs isn't excluded. I wanted to take a different approach with her, though, but I don't know for how long. Her body was sick. I was amazed. I knew she was single, but I didn't care if she had a nigga or not. That shit didn't mean anything to a nigga like me. I could tell she was smart. I'm glad she took the wheel because I was getting tired. She's actually a good driver, though.

I caught a couple hours of sleep. I couldn't stop watching her while she drove. She was so beautiful and pure. I sent her mom a text and told her thank you. I dried off and wrapped a towel around my lower body. I know she didn't get her ass in the bed without me." Yung I blurted out loud wanted her to hear me.

Yung finally decided to get out the shower and come to bed. His phone has been blowing up nonstop, he must have hoe problems. I don't have time for that shit. Let me take my ass to sleep before I throw his phone, I shrugged my shoulders and faced the opposite direction. I don't even know why I should care because we'd just met.

"What you mad for? Did I do something to you? If you mad about my phone you could've answered that shit. What you see is what you get with me. I'm not committed to anybody but this fucking paper I'm chasing. Come here, though, turn around and look at me when I'm talking to you. I see you're hardheaded and I don't like to be ignored."

Yung he threatened her. I picked Killany up and laid her on my chest, her body was soft, and her ass was softer. She was catching feelings already which was good because I wanted her too.

"I'm not mad, why would you assume that? You haven't done anything to me. Who said I wanted to lay on your chest? You're hard headed too," I said. Yung is something else, he's a handful. I don't know what I'm going to do with him. I guess he wanted me just as much as I wanted him. Killany and Yung on the run, I like the sound of it that. Here goes his phone again.

"You want to answer that?" Yung asked. He picked up his phone and gave it to Killany. Let's see what her clap back game is like.

"Hello, who is this? Yes, I'm with Yung tonight. I'm lying on his chest, and he's rubbing on my ass. I'm tracing my tongue on his stomach. Can I help you with something?" I laughed. Whoever was on the other end of the phone was persistent. I didn't mind hurting her feelings either. This trick is blowing her hot ass breath in the phone.

"You got anything that you want to say since you called my phone this late at night, my lil' lady has spoken. I'm trying to dive between her legs, do you want to hear me chew on this pussy?" Yung laughed. Killany was a little wild too. I could tell that we would have fun together. I enjoyed being in her presence; she may be the calm to my storm, this shit is foreign to me. I don't even let women get comfortable with me, but I could get used to this. I know Killany could feel my dick jump, she didn't say anything, though. She was comfortable in her skin, naked and all. Sleep finally took over me, she kept trying to get off of me, I wouldn't let her, though.

Cartier

KC hit me up and told me that Armony was coming to New Orleans. That was cool, but she was bringing Menya in tow. I didn't care, though, Menya already knew what it was. Raven and I were just cool, we just met each other. If it turned out to be something more than that so be it. Menya is a messy chick, but I kept it real with her the whole time. She was just a fuck buddy, and she was cool with that shit. I told her if you see me with another female don't trip, nod your head and keep it pushing, but no she fucked around and caught feelings. She should've been thinking with her pussy and not with her heart. I let Raven know this chick would be here and don't let her make you feel no type of way. I swear if I weren't driving right now I would call and cuss Menya out. The fuck you want to bring your ass down here for. I can see shit going left really quick. I haven't seen her in over a month, Menya was the type of chick that you'll have to put your hands on because she couldn't get the picture.

"Ease up, if your game is as tight as you say it is you have nothing to worry about." Raven laughed. Cartier sweating bullets over there, lame ass. He hasn't told anybody shit, I thought he was a boss, um surely not, we'll see.

"You being funny huh?" He asked. She thinks this shit is funny, she's laughing at me.

Chapter 2

Raven

Kaniya talked me into going away with Cartier for the weekend. Killany was with Yung, so I wouldn't be alone. Cartier and I have been riding for about four hours; we were two hours away when some guy named KC called and said some chick named Menya was coming with Armony who I assumed was his girlfriend. Cartier had the nerve to tell me don't let her make you feel no type way because she's messy.

I know Killany has my back regardless because that's my sister and if not Kaniya will be on a flight, but I got this. If she wanted to fuck with me about a nigga that's not mine, then she would get exactly what she wanted, these motherfucking hands. People assume that because I was quiet that you could fuck me over, not. In my spare time, I box, and nobody knows about it. My manager wants me to do it professionally, but I was focused on school. Don't let this cute face fool you, this ain't what you want, but if you want to beef with me behind a nigga that's not mine or yours then you can get it. I shot Kaniya a text and told her to keep that phone charged I might need bond money.

Raven: *Never leave faces for futures cases, do you need me? If so, I'll catch a flight.*

Kaniya: *No go to bed, why are you up?*

Raven: *Dro.*

Kaniya: *You need to leave him alone.*

Armony

I met KC out here in New Orleans for the weekend, he was waiting for me at the airport when we arrived. He booked us a suite at the Hilton Inn in the French Quarter. I was cool with that, we needed some us time anyway. Menya and I made it about seven PM, KC and I had dinner reservations last night at this nice restaurant on Bourbon Street, and of course, I was dessert. We actually had a good night, just the two of us. Yung and Cartier were here, they brought two chicks with them. KC said they were sisters. Menya will feel like the fourth wheel, but I'll be damned if I let anybody fuck with my girl, sisters or not. We were all scheduled to meet today anyway. I had to see these hoes. I couldn't wait, I shot Menya a text and told her to be extra sexy today, bring that A-Game Jersey in the building.

"Armony, what the fuck are you over there plotting? I know that look in your eyes, and I don't like it. I'm telling you now don't get involved with your so-called friend's mess. I told you to tell her don't come. I don't understand why she would want to get her feelings hurt and come here. Put yourself in her shoes would you do it?" KC asked. Armony thought she was fooling somebody, she couldn't fool me, though. Don't do what Menya does because she's foul, she tried to throw me the pussy on numerous occasions, but I would never cross that line. Armony will find out the hard way what type of friend she is, and it wouldn't have anything to do with me shoving my dick down her throat." KC thought to himself.

"What makes you think I'm up to something? You swear you know me so well, if they try her, then you know I'm going in full force." I chimed in. I couldn't believe KC right now, let me get dressed. The weather was perfect in New Orleans. It was really hot, way warmer than Jersey, I could actually live here.

I had on these white distressed Calvin Klein jeans, a smoke gray blouse that I chose to wear and my Tory Burch thong sandals. KC and I were wearing the same colors. I just washed my hair and blew it out; I was opting for a sleek ponytail today.

Killany

Yung and I just woke up. I can't believe I slept on him the whole night, he had his arms secured around my waist all night. That dick was jumping all night. I had prayed to the good Lord himself last night that my juices wouldn't flow down my legs and I'm glad he answered my prayers because I definitely would've given Yung some pussy on the first night. He was a man of his words, though. I can see that he's a real standup guy. He had his personal consigner here with everything that I could think of, from Victoria's Secret, Balmain, Robin Jeans, Chanel, Gucci, you name it, it was in front of me right now. Yung, I don't need all of this stuff. We're here only for a few days.

"You do you and let me do me. I brought you out here with me, and I told you no bags allowed. You said your birthday was next week and I wanted to get to know you some more, so I knew that you would need extra and your laptop is on its way. I have some business to handle, pick what you like for today and she'll hang the rest up in the closet, get dressed brunch is laid out for you. Welcome to my world." Yung disclosed. I'm as real as they come, He wanted to expose Killany to his life slowly, this will do for now. He has some moves to makes.

Raven

Cartier and I finally made it to New Orleans at about six a.m. this morning. He booked us a suite at the Hilton Inn in the French Quarter. As soon as we made it to the room, I jumped in the shower, and my body made love to the sheets because I was tired. I've never been to New Orleans before, but I've heard plenty of stories. I remember when Katrina hit back in 2005, a lot of the people that lived here moved to Atlanta and I was friends with a lot of them. My first crush was from Louisiana; this guy named Slim. I would never forget him as long as I live, he was fine and chocolate with a gold grill and his accent, oh my God. I loved when he would call me Ray baby, I wonder what ever happened to him, Lord let me stop reminiscing about him. It was after noon, and Cartier and I just woke up. He was sleeping so close to me last night I'm like backup you was just talking fly like I was weak because one of your jump offs was here and you knew she was with the shit. Just because I'm young, quiet and don't say much, don't try me. I'm itching for a bitch to come at me sideways so she can get this work. Killany had sent me a text earlier, I'll hit her back when I get dressed and handle my hygiene.

"I like that smile on your face, you're real beautiful, I was really going to come and find your ass," Cartier stated. Raven is really pretty; I don't think she sees it, she's beautiful, her look is very unique. She's has a real pretty brown complexion when she walks her aura screams fuck me now Cartier. She's about five foot five, with real curly and wavy jet black hair with blonde highlights, a button nose, very nice lips that I would like to see wrapped around my dick and that ass back there is stout, and I can't wait to hit it from the back.

"Yeah right, I don't believe that, but then again it could be true since you have stalker's coming way across the country to be in your presence." I laughed.

"You have your sisters and family fooled, but that innocent look that you have, I'm not buying it. It's more to you, and I want to get to know you some more ma, is that cool?" Cartier asked.

"You sure can, but let me warn you now if we out and some guys try to talk to me don't get in your feelings, ok." I laughed. I was serious too, I heard how Yung was with Killany earlier, and I'm sure the apple doesn't fall far from the tree.

"Let make some shit clear, we are not in a relationship, BUT if you're with me and nigga's try to get at you, I got an issue with that. You don't disrespect me and he won't either, you can do what you want on your time, but not my fucking time. I'm too grown to play games, I'm not sure what you use too, but I'm real about everything I do," Cartier stated. He gave it to Ray straight no chaser. Games will get you killed, fucking with a nigga like me.

"I hear you, I'm about to get dressed, though," I said. I could already see now he's crazy too.

"How come every time I say some shit you don't like you brush everything off? Talk to me, communication is the key, and we need that. I want to get to know you, but if you can't express how you feel it'll never work," Cartier stated. I needed Ray to grow up some and speak her mind. I'm not a psychic and don't want to be one. Tell me what's on your mind.

Yung

KC and I had to handle some business out here that's why we made a short detour. Cartier just got here so he couldn't join us, but I would fill him in on the details later. I just made it back to the room, and Killany was looking good as usual. I liked the way my money looked on her. She was busy on her laptop and phone with what I assumed would be handling business.

I didn't interrupt her. We had lunch with KC, Arm, Cartier, Ray, and Menya in about forty-five minutes. I needed her to wrap things up so we could head over and she could hang with the girls because we needed to handle some business.

"Hey Yung, you back so soon. I'm sorry I was handling business for my clients; a couple of employees had some payroll issues that needed to be corrected. I was able to log in remotely to fix everything, so she should be good within twenty-four hours depending on their financial institutions. What's up with you? You look nice and smell good." Killany laughed. He cleans up really nice.

"Yeah, I had to handle to some business, you don't look bad yourself. You're a business woman, I like the way you handle business, it looks good. Anyways you ready to ride out? We have lunch reservations with KC and his chick, Cartier, and Ray. Leave that desert eagle here, you're not slick." I laughed.

"Oh ok, what if I didn't want to have lunch with them, I just wanted to eat with you and kick it with you?" Killany stated. Kaniya already hit me and said, Ray sent her a text about bond money and some chick that Cartier used to mess with was down there too. As long as she stays in her lane we good, but cross that motherfucker and watch a bitch get real ignorant on your silly ass fucking with my blood.

"You feeling the boss already? We have plenty of time to do whatever you want, trust me." I stated. She wants me, her pussy was so hot last night, she was like a dog in heat. He wanted to give her a taste of this death stroke to cool her off.

"I wouldn't say that just yet, but I could get there, it could get better," Killany said. She liked Yung he's pretty cool, could she get to love him? Yeah, she could see it happening if he plays his cards right. I'll take this shit one day at a time, you never know when a nigga will decide to switch up.

"I'll take that for now, you ready, you got everything you need?" I asked. Killany's pretty cool, He thinks she might be on to something, but women are known to switch up quick.

Chapter 3

Killany

We made our way to Commander's Palace; the restaurant we were scheduled to have lunch at. The scenery was nice; it was located off Washington Ave. I wanted to get me a Grenade to drink. Yung and I were the last ones to show up, I saw Ray. I don't know if she saw how those chicks were grilling her, but I could already tell I was about to Donkey Kong me one of these chicks, don't fuck with mine. Hey, Ray, you miss me, you had to follow me? You good, I don't like the way they're looking at you? Y'all got beef or what?" I blurted. She had to let them chicks know bitch I see y'all and we can get this shit popping.

"I'm good trust me, chill out of course I missed you. I saved you a seat by me. I called you when I woke up you didn't call me back." Raven laughed. She could already tell Killany was on some good bullshit, She's never seen her cut up before, her and Kaniya are one in the same in so many ways.

"I'm Armony, introduce yourself." Armony coaxed. She didn't know who this bitch thought she was. She walked into the room like she owned it and I was beneath her. She could already tell she didn't like her, she can get this work, though.

"I'm Killany, but you can me call me Kill. I'll Kill any and everything moving, you see Ray here that's my blood sister. She looks exactly like me. When you see her, that's all me. If a bitch starts to act ignorant and wants to make some noise with her, I kill it," I boasted. I was talking about with these hands. I'll leave a bitch leaking really quick. I didn't like these hoes' vibes at all. I had to let that shit be known.

"Oh ok, I'm Armony, and I strong arm everything. You see, Menya here is my bitch, and I'm down for her too, like she's my sister. If a bitch got an issue, I'll solve it. I'll strong arm any hoe, even you. Fuck you think this shit is, bitch," Armony divulged. I didn't like that bitch she can get this work today.

"Say less, I'm not one that does too much talking," I vowed. She politely got up out of her seat cracked my knuckles and laid my purse on the table. It was about to get real, I approached the bitch and swung catching ole girl in her mouth.

"Armony chill out do you see where the fuck we at?" KC yelled. I couldn't believe she is acting this way.

"Killany, don't do this shit here," Yung scolded. I couldn't believe she just did that. What's the fucking issue, the two of them don't even know each other?

"Killany! Armony! You two can cut the bullshit. Don't get in between Menya's bullshit. She knows what it is between us, Nothing! We were fucking, and that's it, nothing more, nothing less. Menya why you over there looking stupid and shit. I don't know why in the fuck you came here for what to watch me wine and dine another female that ain't you," Cartier scolded. I couldn't believe this chick don' got all of this shit started. I was very surprised at Raven, she was holding her own. I could see now Killany was evil as fuck, Yung's got his hands full.

"Armony, you know fucking better! Apologize to Killany, you should be ashamed of yourself condoning on some shit that Menya has going on." KC yelled.

"I'm not doing that she was very disrespectful also, I deserve an apology. She just fucking swung on me. I'll apologize after I get my fucking lick back." Armony stated. KC has me all the way fucked up, he knows that shit will never happen.

"Oh, she doesn't have to apologize. I wouldn't accept anyways. I could never respect a bitch that would co-sign for her friend that's in the wrong," I cackled. She better ask about me.

"Killany, ma chill out, please. This ain't the place, you feel me. I understand where you coming from. Ease up, let's eat, and we can be out," Yung whispered. Killany is a firecracker she was ready to dig in Armony's ass.

"Let me say this Cartier, I didn't come here to fuck with you or your new bitch of the week. I came out here because I can, and I do what the fuck I want to do. Nobody can tell me how to move, not even you and the bitch sitting next to you. That tuff shit doesn't scare me think about it. Obviously, you must have some type of feelings for me. You're getting upset, and I haven't even done anything." Menya smirked. I didn't care about what Cartier is saying, it's not over until I says it's over, I, liked what we were doing.

"Excuse me, let me use the restroom really quick, Cartier," Raven shouted. I don't know who Menya thought she was. You won't be calling me a bitch. You and me aren't cool like that, but she was about to wax this hoe. I politely got up, walked past her, dropped my purse on purpose so she would turn around and look. I wanted that bitch to look me in the face when I beat her ass so she could never say that I snuck her and got her from behind. Just like I thought she would, she turned around and gave me the look I was looking for.

I hit that bitch with my right and came back with my left. It was on from there. As soon as she attempted to get up out of her chair, I, jabbed her in the head and punched her in her stomach, and she fell to the floor. She tried to fight back, but she was no match for me. She finally stopped trying to fight me and just took it, I, spat in that bitch's face and walked off.

"Ray, you did that bitch dirty! Arm, let me know if you want this work too. Do y'all see how the fuck my sis is coming? Don't fuck with her, we don't tolerate disrespect at all. You better ask about the fucking Millers we're some fucking Killers. Let's go, Ray, I, didn't want to eat with them. Yung, we'll be at the spot next door," I laughed.

"Ray, come here. Are you good? I'm sorry. I didn't bring you out here for this. I'm sorry she can't get the picture," Cartier pleaded. He couldn't believe Ray was swinging like that. Menya didn't have a chance; that's what the fuck she gets.

"Killany, come here?" Yung yelled. Man, shorty too wild.

"What's up Yung?" I asked. I hope he didn't spit no bullshit. I didn't have time for it. I knew Armony was his peoples and all, but Ray is my sister.

I liked Killany and shit, but I needed a lady. I couldn't believe she cut up the way she did today, I expected a lot more from her. We'll meet you next door," Yung exclaimed. Killany and Ray showed their ass in my boy's spot, people looking at us all crazy and shit.

"But Yung let me explain." I pleaded. That's what I didn't like about Yung he was always judging somebody not knowing the full extent of shit.

"No buts Killany we'll talk about this shit later," Yung yelled. I didn't need her to explain shit. She knew damn well she shouldn't act a fool in public and stoop to Armony and Menya's level. She just had to prove a point.

Chapter 4

Armony

I can't believe these bitches walked up in here like they owned this motherfucker. I won't say that Ray did because she was actually nice. Her sister came in already on go. She wanted to start some shit, and yeah, I was wrong, I shouldn't have instigated. But, that's my friend, I had to have her back.

"Are you ok, Menya?"

This bitch had the nerve to swing on me and hit me in my jaw. I wanted to square up with her.

"Am I ok? Bitch, why in the fuck didn't you jump in? You let this young ass lil' bitch beat the dog shit out of me. She would've never done that to her. You could've at least got her up off of me. That girl could've killed me. You must have been scared of her sister. How could we forgot she knocked you in your jaw and you didn't do shit, lame ass bitch. To make matters worse, you let KC talk to me any kind of way. I don't appreciate that shit. You're foul as fuck, I don't think we can be friends anymore after this. I would've never expected for you to let me go out like this. When that nigga leaves and cheats on you like I know he is, don't fucking call me," Menya yelled. I couldn't believe Armony, I would've never let her go out like that. I had something for her, Yung, KC, Cartier, and Killany: just fucking watch.

"Un-fucking-believable, I can't believe this bitch! The nerve of her to try and blame this shit on me. I told her not to come, true enough I should've jumped in, but for the sake of Yung and KC I didn't jump in or break it up. I have never met a female friend of Yung's. Well, I have, but It wasn't this serious. I could tell by the way he looked at her that he had strong feelings for her already. He looked at her the same way KC looks at me. " I couldn't do shit but shake my head, I didn't even want to hear KC's mouth. It's too late for that.

"Armony, let's go! Fuck her, I'm trying to tell you she's not your friend anyway, you might not see it today, but you'll see it one day." KC yelled. Menya showed her as she flipped on Armony as soon as shit went left. She couldn't even own up to what the fuck she just did.

Raven

Cartier keeps texting and calling me. We are not together, we just met yesterday. I'm telling you, don't fuck with me because I will black out and kill a bitch. Killany doesn't even know the half. Like, before they came, she was saying slick shit about Cartier, about how his dick taste and ask him what her pussy feel like. Armony was laughing, being messy, I was laughing too because the bitch was being silly. I had Kaniya and my momma on FaceTime and they were lit as fuck telling me don't let no bitch disrespect me.

"Ray Ali, you good? You quiet over there? I need you to fill me in the next time you want to kickbox a bitch. I wanted to mop the floor with Arm, whatever the chick name was. You see I came in on go mode. Your sneaky little ass is a fucking plotter, I don't like your Kaniya tendencies," Killany laughed. Raven showed her motherfucking ass, her whole approach was slick as fuck. She liked the way she moved with that one.

"Girl whatever, I know you aren't talking. You walked up in that bitch like you was Nicki Minaj, and Yung was Jeezy and some shit. You make me sick. Your mouth was so slick, If that was me I would've reached across the table and smacked fire from your ass. Call me Kill, I kill everything moving, you are too much," I laughed. Killany isn't that bad once you get to know her, she's ghetto too, I couldn't believe how ratchet she got. I should've recorded her so Kaniya could see, she wouldn't believe this shit.

Cartier

Raven surprised the fuck out of me with this shit that she pulled. I promise you I didn't think that she had that shit in her. I thought she was soft and weak, but I knew she was sneaky and I said earlier that she didn't fool me. Menya deserved that shit. Ray was nice, she spoke to them the moment she sat down. Menya was on some straight bullshit. Armony was wrong for that too. I'm glad Killany busted her in her mouth. If she knew that Menya offered KC the pussy, I bet she wouldn't be going this hard for her. Since she left the restaurant, she's been blowing up my phone, begging me to shove my dick down her throat. Bitch don't you see me with somebody, miss me with that little bullshit. I have to apologize to Ray he should've stopped Menya before she got started. I know a nigga was in the dog house because she's not even answering her phone or texts. I have to make this shit right.

"You fucked up good CJ, I told you about fucking with Menya, but you didn't want to listen, that bitch is poison you'll see." Yung laughed. CJ swears he's a player and his game is tight as fuck.

"You hard headed, you just had to go against the grain." KC, he needs to listen to what a motherfucker tells him. That bitch is crazy, and he has to find out the hard way.

KC

I'm so pissed with Armony. If I tell you to do something, you need to fucking do it. I told her to leave Menya at home because I knew this shit would happen. It has blown up in her face. I don't trust Menya, something is up with her besides trying to throw the pussy at me. Armony's so blind she can't even see that this bitch is jealous of her. If I could record this bitch and show Armony she still wouldn't recognize it.

"I'm sorry KC," Armony stated. She should've just listened to him instead of trying to be down for my girl, for her to turn around and flip this shit on me. Look, she's already ranting on Facebook talking about what happened.

"Armony, I've told you so many times Menya doesn't mean you any good. I won't tell you how, but you need to sit back, pay attention, and observe shit. Everybody is not your friend. You're smart as fuck, but I refuse to let you fall victim to her bullshit." If I tell Armony the real reason why Menya is foul she'll be ready to kill her. I needed her to be able to spot snakes from a mile away. Armony is very smart, but she ignores a lot of shit. I need her to be twenty- twenty about everything.

"Is that Yung's new girlfriend? I don't like her at all, she was rude as fuck. Ole girl that Cartier was fucking with had some nice hands, her quiet ass served Menya that work. I promise you I didn't think that she had it in her. It's not good to judge a book by its cover."

That's what Menya gets, she kept picking with that girl for no reason at all. Killany will see me again. "Armony said.

"I don't know, he just met her yesterday. Menya deserved that ass whooping, she kept fucking with shorty. I think that she would've whooped Cartier's ass too, she blacked out" KC laughed.

Chapter 5

Raven

Killany and I ate at this restaurant a few doors down called The Joint, it was really nice. The food was good, it had a Bistro feel to it. I grabbed the grilled Cajun catfish, rice pilaf, shrimp, and asparagus it was really good. We were having a good time until Cartier and Yung came over. I guess Cartier could sense the tension; I really didn't have an issue with him. My issue was if you brought me here, why did you let that shit go down. I didn't ask to come, you knew this chick was messy, you should've stopped her in her fucking tracks. Since she wanted to keep that bullshit going, shit got real. So know I don't have no words for Cartier, none at all.

"Laila Ali, you good? Can I borrow your sister for the rest of the night? Let's go Killany." Yung laughed. Cartier is in the fucking dog house. I promise you I didn't think she had it in her, but her eyes are cold.

"Ray, I'm going to slide up out of here. I love you, and I'll see you tomorrow," I kissed, Ray on her cheek, that's my lil' hitter she got some hands on her.

"No, you won't see her tomorrow or the next day," Yung stated. I needed Killany to myself for the next couple of days.

"Excuse me Killany, I like Yung he just might be the one to tame your stuck-up ass, you are obeying him too; not even putting up a fight. "Raven laughed. Killany met her match. Although I've only known her for a short period of time, I've grown to love her. She's rude and obnoxious. If you didn't know her, you would swear she was stuck up. She didn't like me at first because I was the youngest and she was a daddy's girl. I didn't want the position; I was just glad to know that I had some sisters.

"Hey shorty, you good? I shot you a text, and you didn't hit me back. I'm sorry," Cartier said. She was ignoring the hell out of me. He hoped this one thing doesn't change what they could possibly have.

"We're good, the only issue that I have is she kept picking with me. I didn't say shit because I didn't feel like I had to and you didn't say shit either. I did what I had to do, I don't tolerate disrespect at all. You brought me here, I know we aren't together, but it's just the principal. She didn't know her place, and I wasn't stepping on her toes, we just met," I stated. To be honest, I didn't know if I wanted to fuck with Cartier after this. Menya was crazy, and the shit that she did was too much. I was cool on him, this whole little situation is fucking up anything we could've ever had. I didn't need the extra drama.

Cartier

I can't even be mad at shorty right now I understood everything she just said. I was just telling her don't ever disrespect me, and I just straight let Menya disrespect her. If it's meant to be then, we will be. I feel like shit right now, my momma would kill me if she knew what just transpired. We were headed back to our room. She was in her phone the whole time, laughing and shit. I wanted to laugh, too. I just chose not to say anything right now. She had a beautiful smile.

"What's funny Raven, talk to me."

"I'm trying to finish this book that I was reading, it's really good," Raven stated. It's called She's My Forever, He's My Eternity by Ashley Robinson.

"Oh, I thought you were laughing at me," I said. *She's probably lying. I know that book isn't that funny.*

"Why would I be laughing at you? What did you do that was so funny?" Raven asked. He needs to shut up and drive, she didn't like being interrupted while she was reading.

"I was just making sure. I really am sorry about earlier, I feel like shit. Please don't judge me off of this little situation." I pleaded.

"You good, I'm not even on that anymore. I forgive you, don't let that shit happen ever again not just to me, but anybody." Raven stated. I couldn't believe he's still thinking about that shit.

"Ok cool it won't happen anymore. Do you have anything in

mind that you want to do while we are out here?" I asked.

Yung

Killany and I stayed in New Orleans for a few extra days, it was cool and shit. We went to the casino and balled the fuck out. I think she was my good luck charm, I won twenty thousand on the crap tables, she blew on the dice, and it was on from there. I gave her fifteen thousand just because. She refused to take it, but I stuffed it in her bag. Cartier and Raven left yesterday, she actually flew back because Cartier was a making a detour. He wasn't going straight back to Atlanta, he had to handle some business in Mississippi, and she had to get back for school. KC and Armony left two days ago.

Killany and Armony couldn't get along for shit. It was too much tension, so I was glad that they were leaving anyway. I wouldn't stress it too much as of right now, but if Killany planned on rocking with me, her and Armony had to squash the bullshit they had going on because they would be in each other's presence often. Killany's birthday was next Friday, she mentioned something about her and her sister having a nineties party, a birthday dinner or some shit.

I was a selfish as nigga when it comes to my needs and wants. I didn't want her to leave, not yet anyway. I needed her to stay, she had everything she needed to kick it with me for a few weeks or a month. The moment she sat in the passenger seat of my car it was no coming back. I had some business to handle out in Vegas. I booked us a suite at Trump International Hotel. After I finalize this last situation, I was headed back to Jersey to chill out for a few. I needed her to be on board with going to Vegas.

"Hey Killany, do you want to go to Vegas for a week? It'll be an early birthday gift?"

"Of course, when are we leaving?" Killany asked.

Chapter 6

Killany

When I first laid eyes on Yung, I knew he was the one for me. I could tell he was a real savage, I knew I had to have him. I was caught up between him and his brother Cartier, but something was telling me to go for Yung he was the one. It's hard to explain, the feelings that I felt towards him were very different and to be honest, I was scared of that shit. It was very magical, and it's like my soul was telling me that he was the one. The way his hazel eyes pierced my soul, and his Creed cologne invaded my nostrils.

I remember our first encounter like it was yesterday. Yung and I had a miscommunication, he passed judgment on my sister, and I didn't like that. I didn't want to pursue him just because he had something to say about my sister. Our relationship started off so fast I wouldn't put a title on what we have yet. He was my savage, and I was his rider if need be. These past few months we've been connected at the hip. I didn't even get to spend my birthday with my sister. Yung booked us a flight to Vegas, and I spent my birthday there. I've been dating Yung for about a month now, and life has been great so far. He's actually everything that I've ever wanted and needed in a man.

Yung came into my life when I was very vulnerable and desperate to be loved. I've had my fair share of guys, nothing to rave about. My savages, my savages, every time I heard that song by FUTURE I thought about Yung. He came into my life unexpectedly; I still couldn't get over how we met. My mom introduced us, I was against it at first because I didn't want her hooking me up with anybody. I was capable of finding my own man. I was actually more than ready to leave Atlanta, the timing was perfect, but so many secrets and other shit were coming out.

The only thing positive that came to play the few weeks that I was out there was meeting Ray, my sister and meeting Yung, my savage. He was the realest guy that I've ever met besides my dad. This man was so sexy to me it didn't make any sense.

He was six foot two, caramel complexion, built super nice, bottom grill, with hazel eyes and his body, was covered with tats. He has a nice beard and pretty teeth. He was a real street nigga. He walked, talked, and woke up like a boss. Every day he lived his life to the fullest, and since we've been kicking it pretty hard, he made sure that I've done the same. The one thing that stood out about him the most was he was a fucking savage. This man was A1 in everything that he did. Men and women feared him in the streets, but that shit didn't impress me at first, though. I was looking for something different. I was looking for my ride or die. I wanted a man like my father. My father always told me that my mother was his true rider. She had his back when nobody didn't, he hates that she was the one that got away. My father told me that once you find that one true love you'll know and to never let him go no matter the circumstances.

I didn't want an average street nigga. I was looking for my Clyde because I damn sure was Bonnie and I was down to ride for mine until the very end. When Yung came into my life I wasn't looking for love I was looking for a check. He was used to women wanting him for his money, but I had my own.

Yung

I promise you I was falling for Killany something serious. She's my rider, she's down for the kid. She came into my life when I thought love was foreign. Don't get me wrong I've had my fair share of women, but there was something special and different about Killany. I wanted to get to know her more. Her aura and demeanor spoke volumes she was five foot three, caramel brown, with deep cheekbones, pretty teeth with two gold fangs in her grill. Her ass was fat, and her breasts were nice, perky, and suckable; she was thick as fuck. I could tell she was cornbread fed. She didn't care too much for bundles or extensions, she wore her natural hair really wild and really curly. Her walk was deadly, and she commanded attention; she kept mine from the moment I laid eyes on her.

The way she was holding that Desert Eagle when we first met had me rock hard. I could tell she had a story and it was more to her than a pretty face. I met her through her momma, I remember that shit like it was yesterday. The thought of our first encounter will forever be etched in my mind. Don't get me wrong you know how some mothers brag about their kids. Mrs. Kaisha was the same way, she told Cartier and me that her daughters were the truth and nobody was fucking with them on their worst day. I had to see Kaniya and Killany.

She invited us to a cookout and told us they would be attendance. I went through, and when my eyes landed on Killany, I knew I had to have her. We exchanged numbers, and we sent text's to each other the whole time while we were at the cookout. I really enjoyed her conversation. I needed more than that from her. I wanted to kick it and see if she could spit some good game in person instead of behind her iPhone. I asked her to run away with me. To my surprise, she didn't object she's been connected at my hip ever since.

I didn't see myself falling for Killany at all. You know how they say opposites attract, that's how it was for us. I was attracted to Killany from the first time I saw her. What I loved the most about her was she didn't look at me for what I had and what I could do for her. She had her own. We crossed that line already, but I wanted more from her than just sex. I wanted to build something with her. I'm not sure if she's ready, I know she's gutta, I watched her tote a pistol. At the same time, my life is complicated and loving a savage ain't easy. I need a ride or die. When shit gets complicated, I don't need her to fold under pressure. I don't know if she's capable of doing that. She can protect herself, but I need her to protect me and her if need be. I was going to ask her again tonight if she was ready because I was tired of this dating shit. She thinks she slick. I know she still be shooting texts to different cats. If she thought that she could run game on me like her sister was running game on niggas. She had me fucked up and sadly mistaken.

Armony

Let me introduce myself my name is Armony Luciano and I'm twenty-seven years old. I've been dating the infamous Kanan KC Alibumbiyae. We've been dating each other for three years now. I was crushing hard on KC something serious and when we first met it was magical. He stayed on my mind constantly. I knew KC was the one for me when I first laid eyes on him and he captivated my attention. I own a shoe boutique; it's located right inside The Mills at Jersey Gardens it's an Italian pizza shop; Julian's that's not too far from my spot. I ordered some Manicotti; that's my favorite.

I was paying for my food, and I accidentally bumped into him by mistake as I was leaving. He wrapped his arms around my waist to keep me from falling, and he felt me up, damn I was wet on sight. My pussy was tingling from his touch. His Tom Ford cologne hypnotized my nostrils. I wanted that moment to never end, it could've lasted forever. His eyes pierced through my soul. It felt so right in his arms. This man was sent from heaven; six foot four, caramel brown, solid muscles, goatee, body covered in tats, low fade, nice teeth, deep waves, and dimples. Two hundred forty pounds with big brown eyes and that big loaf in between his legs. I love it when he baptizes me with that big loaf. Dick so good you'll sell your soul to the devil, I promise you. I called him KC the Baptist, every time I hop on that dick I commit a sin. I'm ready to carry his last name; my parents love him to death.

KC

Let me introduce myself if Armony hasn't already. I'm twenty-eight years old, I'm a Scorpio, and I'm a street nigga by heart and by choice. I reside in Newark, NJ, I was born in Atlanta, but I was raised and got paid in Jersey. I run my father's empire; the infamous Alibumbiyae. I have my right-hand Yung assisting me, and I have my left-hand Cartier assisting me with shit. I don't know my mother, she's a deadbeat bitch, and If I ever meet her, I'll spit in her face. She left my dad and me to fend for ourselves, but I was good. My aunt Amber raised me and uncle Taliyae and my dad raised and bred me to be the most thorough nigga out here in these streets.

I never longed for my mother or even thought to look for her, she said fuck me, so it's always fuck her. No matter the circumstances, fuck her. It's only one woman that has my heart and its Armani Luciano; she has my soul, and she'll be the only woman to carry my last name and bare my kids. I was digging Armony long before our first encounter. I always frequented Julian's; the pizza shop next to her shoe Boutique. I was sitting in my car waiting for a call before I went inside to pick up some money. I noticed her stature through the window of her shop, it's a very nice setup. Her hips had me hypnotized, and her pecan brown skin glistened when she moved, and the way her ass was sitting up in those jeans and breast were sitting up like fluffy pillows, I knew I had to have her. She thinks that our first encounter was our first time meeting, but I went to Julian's every day just to see her. I knew she was made for me way before she even laid eyes on me. She was my prey, and I staked claim to her. That was three years ago, and we're still rocking super hard.

Chapter 7

Killany

Yung and I just finished having breakfast in bed. He was eating me, and I was sucking on him. I was quite full, we had to hurry up and get dressed he has a business meeting at the warehouse, and he wanted me to come with him. We finally put a title on this thing that we have here. I didn't feel like doing anything. I just wanted to lay around and do nothing, mainly because I wasn't interested in keeping company with KC's fiancé or whatever, but for the sake of my man I'll play nice only for today. After this meeting, Yung and I are supposed to go house shopping. He insists that I move in with him. I think we're moving too fast, he says the pace is perfect. He doesn't want to do the long-distance thing.

I told him that we don't have to we can be friends and continue how we are. He had a fit, Yung thought he was slick I knew he was going in my phone after I went to sleep. I didn't put a lock on it because I had nothing to hide. I was kicking it heavy with this guy name Kingston before Yung and I confirmed what we were doing. We used to go out on dates at least twice a week.

He was actually a cool guy, and I loved to hang out with him, but he was just keeping me occupied until Yung figured out what he wanted to do. He would shoot me texts here and there telling me good morning, he missed me, and he wanted to see me when I touchdown. I would reply back, we would have regular conversation. I knew Yung was going through my phone because when I would check my messages, his message would be deleted as if no conversation was ever there, that shit was so hilarious. Watch this shit; Yung you've been going through my phone? I had to ask him to see what his response was going to be.

"Yeah I went through your shit! Why in the fuck are you still having conversations with another man if you're with me? Part of being with me you can't have a conversation with any niggas outside of your dad and my niggas, no interaction period understand that shit Killany." Yung said. Who in the fuck did I think he was. I don't care if yawl were friends or not, but he's not my friend so no you can't text him. He's begging to see my woman and telling her good morning and shit. That didn't sit right with me. Call me petty, but I texted him back and told him to lose her number if he didn't want any problems, she's in a relationship.

"Do I go through your stuff Yung? I respect your privacy, but you want to invade mine. Give me your phone since you're calling shots, all four of them. I'm sure it's some chicks texting you. That's what I thought who is Tiffany and Kyla? These hoes asking you when are you coming back through kissy face emoji. Yung, you got me fucked up, clear this shit up now and not on the phone take me to these hoes so I can verify this shit." I said. I didn't know who he thought he was, please don't let this cute face fool you. Ain't shit weak about me, I felt the need to address these hoes, and you face to face, I don't chin check over the phone. He knew I was crazy he saw me cut up in New Orleans.

"Calm down Killa I'm not checking for nobody, but you. We can tell these chicks face to face with you on my arm to stop hitting me up. I'm exclusive with you, I meant what the fuck I said about you and conversations with that cat in your phone. Hurry up and get dressed I got your clothes out already. Put some fucking panties on too, you think you're slick. I noticed how your ass jiggles when you're not wearing any, don't fucking try me today." Killany just thinks she laid down the law. She got me bricked up how she just came at me talking reckless and shit.

"I don't know who Yung thought he was. He always wants to pick out my clothes and dress me up like I'm his personal Barbie and shit. I'm capable of picking out my own shit he always wants us to dress alike. I don't like wearing all black every day, I like to wear different colors. Ugh, I'm pissed just thinking about this shit. My dad doesn't even handle me the way Yung tries to." I thought to myself. He got me fucked all the way up, the panty and bra set he left out will not be worn. I got something for him. He better not even makes an attempt to get in the shower with me.

"Killany, look at me when I'm talking to you. We are not doing this petty shit, get that mug up off your face and lose your attitude and the panty's and bra you left on the bed you can get that shit too, don't fucking trying me. Don't put it on and watch me put it on you." Yung said. Killany is the type of chick that you have to man handle. I have to get all up in her face and man handle her. I hate to do it, but it has to be done. She really has an attitude like she wasn't entertaining that nigga, not one time did she tell him she was in a relationship. I didn't respond back to none of those chicks. If she wanted to check them to prove a point, I was going to let her do just that.

Chapter 8

KC

Meanwhile on the other side of town...

I had a meeting with Yung and Cartier today out East. We had some new product coming in that needed to be tested out. I had to pull down on Kilgore so he can come and taste it for me. He has a good tongue to taste for pure coke and he would let me know on site what I was working with. Armony was coming with me and Yung was bringing Killany. It's important that the two of them get along because Yung and I where on one accord and we needed them to fall in line. Armony was fine with it, she didn't fool with too many females, but she had one friend Menya the African chick that I didn't trust. They haven't been kicking it heavy like they used to since the little situation with Raven that happened in New Orleans. Cartier used to bust her down some months ago.

Killany was antisocial, but she was cordial. She couldn't fool me though anytime a chick walks around with a desert eagle in her bag ain't shit shy or friendly about you. One thing that I love about Armony the most is she's adapted to change. If I need her ride out she's down no questions asked. It's always baby what you need me to do and she suit's or vest's up, but I didn't want her out here in these streets like that, she's my most prized possession.

"Babe, what are you thinking about, you're in deep thought?" Armony asked. KC was in deep thought about something. I didn't like my man thinking too much or too long or stressing about nothing.

"I'm good I was just thinking about all the shit we have to do today. I want to take you out on date tonight. I was thinking about going to New York for the weekend, what do you think?" I inquired. I know she's down to go, no questions asked, but her store has been bringing in a lot of business. She might not want to close up shop for a few days.

"Yes baby, I'm ready should I go ahead and pack my bag now or what? Yung and Killany are they coming also?" Armony asked. I haven't been to New York in a month or so. Hell yeah, I was down to go. I could shop my ass off and get some more stuff for my store too.

"Baby you never need a bag. You're always good. I don't know if Yung and Killany are coming. It's your weekend, it's all about you. You can invite them if you want. If not, me and you are riding out regardless." I said. I love Armony, you see my baby is always thinking of others.

"Hurry up and get dressed babe so we can leave. I picked your clothes out already; socks, boxers, and everything even the cologne. I'm cooking you breakfast so you won't have an excuse to stop." Armony said. I make sure KC is good every day, all day. If he wanted me to cook him lunch every day I would close my shop up every day at noon to do so.

"Damn baby you on it." I said. I'm blessed to have a woman like Armony.

Killany

We were finally where leaving Yung's condo to head to his warehouse. It was dark and gloomy; it had just finished raining. He just had to jump in his Aston Martin. I told him it was too flashy; he needs some low-key shit. It was about thirty minutes away. New Jersey was a very beautiful state; it was pretty cool even though I was with Yung every day. I still missed home though. I actually wanted to go back to Atlanta to be up under my mom, Ray, and Kaniya. I would rather lay up under Yung any day, the way his chest is cut up he's like my personal body pillow. I've gotten so used to lying up under him it's ridiculous. My mom says I'm the next one that's going to be pregnant, unlike Kaniya I'm on the shot. I'll treat her kids just like my own.

"Killany, what are you thinking about? Your mind is somewhere else and not focused on me." Yung stated. Killany got that sneaky ass look on her face likes she's up to something. I saw that same look on Kaniya's face at the fucking cookout.

"Yung shut up, if you must know I'm thinking about you and your wild ass. Is it a problem?" I asked. He's so damn nosey it's ridiculous. If it's not Yung's way, it's no way.

"I'm right here baby, you don't have to keep your thoughts to yourself. You can tell me what's on your mind we don't have nothing but time." Yung said. I needed Killany to understand that she can talk to me about whatever. He's here for her no matter what.

"I was thinking about you, K, Ray, and my mom. Nothing too much to dwell on but your chest is my body pillow, I don't want to give it up. "I laughed. I knew that wasn't the answer that Yung was looking for, but that's all he was getting for now.

"Kill it Killany man you can't even be serious. That's all you were you thinking about? Just admit that you love a nigga and you were thinking about how I put this dope dick up in you and you be hollering all night. Yung stop, slow down, aww right there." Yung I shot back at Killany really quick. She plays all day, we finally made it to the warehouse. KC hasn't made it yet, late ass nigga. I'll go ahead and go in and get started. Everything looks in place and intact.

"Hopefully this won't take too long, I can go in Yung's office and do some work. It's so fucking cold in here, this office is a fucking mess. This man forgets that I have a job and clients that I attend to also. Kaniya emailed me twice, she wanted me to review some contracts. She had some new investors and clients that want her to do direct hiring for them." I thought to myself. This shit will take all day and this contract is very thick and it has a ton of clauses included.

"Hi Killany, what's up girl how you been?" Armony stated. I should run up on this bitch and knock her in her fucking jaw while she's not looking. This bitch swears she's busy, she's probably on Facebook or Instagram. Let's see if she has some smart shit to say. I hope she got past that shit in New Orleans.

"Hi Armony, I'm good and you? I'm working on a few things. Feel free to have a seat." I advised. I hoped this bitch don't get on my nerves, saved by FaceTime. Ugh Kaniya's about to trip.

"Killany damn can you stay up off of Yung's dick and at least look at the shit I've sent you? I love your glow and all, but business before dick. Let me see what you got on, you're cute or whatever looking like me and shit, minus the belly, where you at?" Kaniya asked. Killany's slipping she needs to tighten up. She can't even do the small shit that I need her to do.

"Hold up Kaniya, watch how you talk to me. Can I get a hey, how are you or something? I'm looking at everything you sent me right now. I'm at the dungeon with Yung. You wish I looked like your ratchet ass." I laughed. Kaniya needs to pump her brakes, rushing me to do shit won't speed up the process.

"Fuck you Killany Denise, bitch you get some new dick and don't know how to act. Where Yung at so I can ask him what that mouth do? Who is that with you laughing bitch, when you get some friends? Let me find out, make me come and see about you." Kaniya said. She's a trip she's acting all brand new and shit.

"It's Armony; KC's fiancé. Say hi to my imposter." I chuckled. I hope Kaniya doesn't say nothing slick to this girl, I know how she is.

"Hi Kaniya! Killany didn't tell me she was a twin. She never mentioned you just Raven." Armony admitted. This bitch didn't tell me she had a twin. Her sister is lit as fuck.

"Hi you're pretty. Let me introduce myself I'm Kaniya; Killany's twin it's nice to meet you. Excuse my behavior, I miss my boo she left me for some dick. Killany, I love you, I miss you, hit me back later." Kaniya stated. I had to get off FaceTime before I said some slick ass shit to Armony about fucking with Raven even though that issue was solved already.

"I didn't know you're a twin; double trouble." Armony stated. That's pretty cool, her sister was gorgeous.

"It's a lot you don't know about me." I said. Ugh, here she goes being nosey and shit. Stay out of my business and mind your own.

"Look Killany, I'm not going nowhere and neither are you. We're fucking with two bosses whose bond can't be broken. This static that you're giving me you can kill it because whether we like it or not. We'll be seeing a lot of each other so we have to form some type of bond." Armony informed her. I'm so sick of her stuck-up ass. I'm not pressed for friends, but I'm just letting her know at the end of the day I'll let KC know I tried and I'm not trying anymore. I don't kiss ass, never have and never will. I don't lose sleep.

"I hear you Armony. I just don't trust females like that. It's always been me and my sister, now I have another sister. I'm willing to get to know you, but Menya is a no go. It's something about her that I don't trust or like. Watch her and keep her from around me." I said. Lord I feel like I just sold my soul to the devil. I'll try it, Armony isn't that bad. She let it be known that she wasn't going anywhere and that we needed to bond regardless.

"I'm glad that you're on board because I brought Vaseline today and we could square up because your attitude stinks. I need to get my lick back, but I guess I won't need it after all. Everybody says the same thing about Menya, I need to sit back and observe. KC and I are headed to NY this weekend, you two should join us." Armony said. It's about time she got it together because bitch we could've fought today. I'll square up with anybody, even you.

"Armony, do you hear that? Come and look at the surveillance system Yung and KC are getting robbed are you strapped?" I yelled. They got mine fucked up. I'm glad I looked up and saw what was going on.

"What the fuck are you waiting on? I'm always strapped, open the safe and grab the two AR 15'S and a bullet proof vest and let's go." Armony yelled. I'm calling the shots today, I be damn if anybody think they can take from KC and live to tell about it. My man works too hard and I'm about to show these pussies how hard in the paint I go for him.

Chapter 9

Killany

I just got Yung in my life and I for damn sure wasn't about to lose him to some fucking jack boys. I'm about to make a mess, it's ten fuck boys. I'm dropping five and I need Armony to drop the other five. Let's go! You go left and I'm going to the right! No faces, no cases you feel me." Killany stated. I gave Armony the rundown. Let's see if she's about that action. Who would want to rob Yung and KC? The day that I wanted to wear some Timberlands this man picked me out some fucking Red Bottoms. Look at me, now I guess I have to kill in heels. I walked smoothly across the pavement in the warehouse. I didn't want my heels to click, I didn't want to alert intruders. Where's his fucking security? I don't see anybody around.

I spotted Yung and the nigga that was trying to rob him. He had a gun pointed to his back and somebody else had one to his head. They were brave as hell, no masks at all. I lined the scope up to make sure I had a good aim on my target. I used the desert eagle on him because it had a silencer on it; the other guys weren't paying attention. He was not about to take out my man, not today. I tucked that desert eagle behind my back and placed the Ar-15 on my shoulder getting prepared to shoot, I wanted nothing but headshots. I had to serve these pussies to my nigga on the platter. My adrenaline was already rushing from just dropping one body. I hit my fourth target dead in the head. Yung just flinched, blood got on him and I dropped the next two the same way. My final target tried to run, I lit his ass up.

Armony

I lived for this shit, I was a trained assassin. I'm glad I opted out for a Pink jogging suit today and some Nike Air Maxes. I put my headphones on, I had Jeezy playing It Ain't No Other Way. I made my way over towards KC, two guys were holding him at gun point my baby was not about to lose his life today. I was so good at throwing knives; it's a skill that I mastered very well. My first target had his back turned so he couldn't see me, but I eyed him very well.

I threw the knife at his skull, it landed in the middle of his head, he turned around and I let that AR rip the other guy that had KC. He attempted to shoot back, but his Aim was off. I had the scope positioned on him so good he never moved from his position and I unloaded straight lead, dead in his chest. I tossed KC the extra AR and he handled the other three, him and Yung. I had to get them cowards up off of my baby.

"Killany bring your ass over here now." Yung's voice boomed. Me and KC had this shit under control this spot is armed. We were playing with these suckas to see who sent them, and got them sent out, but no Thelma and Louise had to set this shit off like the fourth of July. Now we don't know nothing. I appreciate her for riding for me and shit, but damn you wiped everybody out without blinking one fucking eye. I told her about carrying that desert eagle every fucking where.

"I don't know who Yung thought he was, handling me like that.

He's not Killian Miller so I was ignoring his ass and walked over to Armony and KC, fuck him and his attitude." Killany thought to herself.

"Armony never seems to amaze me, my baby girl was at these niggas necks. She didn't ask no fucking questions. She's proved her loyalty to me on more than one occasion. I was glad she was here, she swears I'm the trap god and she's my trap queen. I don't want that for her though. Killany was letting that shit rip, she sprayed that last nigga. Yung was pissed for some reason, he needs to get over that shit and go console his girl to make sure she's straight." KC thought to himself.

"Killany, are you straight girl? You got a nice aim, girl. I couldn't believe you were moving so swift with those Red Bottoms. We make a good team, you're a real rude girl with your steel." I smiled. I couldn't believe Killany was shooting like that her aim is nice as fuck. It is a lot of shit that I don't know about her.

"Bring your trap queen ass on Armony, fucking up my place of business." KC yelled. She walked over to me all sexy with a smirk on her face. I picked her up bridal style and kissed her passionately on her lips and carried her to my office.

"You heard me talking to you, don't you ever dismiss me when I tell you to do something. That's your problem now, you're hard headed and didn't I tell you about carrying that desert eagle on you. Come here ma, what If something would've happened to you doing that hot ass shit, Killany." Yung argued. This girl would be the death of me. I appreciated her and shit, but damn she stays on some hot girl shit.

"I wasn't thinking about me Yung, I was thinking about you. I didn't want a pussy to play you so no I'm never going to be cautious when fucking you. If you're in some shit and it's looking skeptical I'm doing me. Killing everything moving straight up and I'm not remorseful about that. I'm going to go home for a few days we need some time apart" Killany warned. I couldn't believe him right now.

"Oh, that's how you feel do you need to grab anything by the house? The car door is open get your ass in. You booked a flight already?" Yung argued. I didn't know who Killany thought she was. He was the man in the relationship so she needs to follow. If she wanted to run her ass to Virginia because she's in her feelings, then I was going to let her. I'm not running behind her, but I knew one fucking thing she better not entertain King, she'll be his fucking demise. I already told that nigga.

"No, I don't need anything. I'll buy a ticket when I get to the airport." Killany taunted. I didn't give a fuck about his attitude, he doesn't appreciate shit. Instead of him being loving and caring like KC he wants to bitch and gripe. I don't have time for that, let me go home. My phone alerted me that I had a text

Armony: *Yawl good?*

Killany: *Fuck Yung I'm going home! I'm headed to the airport now he is in his feelings, give him a tampon when you see him. Lol!*

Armony: *You stupid, you'll be back in two days. Yung is falling for you trust me I know.*

Killany: *Whatever.*

"You here, where are you going to Atlanta or Virginia?" Yung asked. She better not come with no slick shit.

"Jamaica for a few days, I'll see you though." Killany joked. Don't clock my moves. I'll dip on his ass quick and get some passport stamps and a tan.

"Killany, don't make me hurt you! Stop fucking playing where are you going?" Yung warned. I knew she was on some slick shit.

"Atlanta Yung, is it a problem." Killany revealed. How fast he was driving I didn't think he would care where I was going. I miss my sister so I wanted to go lay in her bed and vent about this fool.

"Oh, alright give me a kiss." Yung said. I made sure he tongued the fuck out of her, she wanted to leave and run her ass off I was going to make sure I gave her ass something to miss. Let me call Kaniya so she can text me when she touches down.

"What Yung, what the fuck you do to my sister? Make me come to Jersey and wipe your ass clean the fuck out about mine." Kaniya inquired. He got me messed up behind Killany's stubborn ass.

"Shut the fuck up and spit that hot ass shit to your baby daddies. I didn't do shit she's stubborn and you know that. She's on the way though, she's in her feelings about some shit that just happened and I guess she wanted me to baby her like KC does Armony, but I'm not that nigga, so I don't move like him." Yung hinted. I had to give her the run down.

"Oh yeah, she's very stubborn I'll holla at her about that though. I'll hit you when I pick her up." Kaniya said. I can only imagine the type of hell Killany puts Yung through. She has been blowing my phone wanting to vent, I didn't want to hear it.

Chapter 10

Yung

I love Killany I really do, but I don't want her killing niggas without consequences. I should've apologized to her, but my pride wouldn't allow it me to do it. I had a serpent in my circle, and I wanted to know who the culprit was. I love that Killany is down for whatever and I understand where she was coming from, but it's more to it. We brought the girls here on purpose to see if any fuck shit would pop off. I knew whoever was trying to set us up thought that because the girls were here, we wouldn't be focused because the girls would be a distraction. They thought wrong because Killany and Armony together is a disaster waiting to happen, I just witnessed that. I knew Killany was a little hood, but damn she's on a whole different level she has some serious skills. Mrs. Kaisha didn't lie when she said nobody was fucking with her daughter. I was in a trance when she clipped ole boy in front me and he didn't even see it coming. Where did she get a silencer from? She played her position, I hate that I don't have any answers. I hate that she felt the need to run off to Atlanta instead of discussing shit with me first.

Armony

KC and I were still at the warehouse. The clean-up crew hasn't arrived yet. I just sent a text Killany to see if she was good. I noticed Yung's attitude, I didn't care for it at all. I actually liked Killany for Yung, she's the best I've seen thus far besides the other women that he kept company with. I can tell she's a cool chick once you get to know her. I wanted her to come to New York with us.

"KC, Killany said that she was on her way home. Yung was in his feelings, so now they won't be joining us in New York."

"Yung has a pride issue; he wants to be in control of everything. I know him better than he knows himself. He doesn't like the fact that Killany bodied five niggas and he didn't have to help. I hate to say it, but he will fuck around a miss a good thing before it happens. I'm finished in here, are you ready to go? I want to get on the road before it gets too dark. Lock it up, and I'm going to do another walk through," KC said. I needed to holla at Yung on some real shit about Killany. He's so blinded by other shit he can't see that she's the one. Even Ray Charles can see that shit.

Killany

I had to get away from Yung, he hurt my feelings, and he got me in my feelings. I should've never let my guard down, but I did. I was willing to give us a try, despite my doubts I was willing to take a chance. He didn't stop me or console me. I was just being me that's all I can be. I'll always shoot first and ask questions later regardless the circumstances. I'll deal with the consequences later my flight was about to land anyway. I'm not going back to New Jersey I'll stay out here for a week and then I'll go to Virginia. I don't give a fuck what Kaniya has going on, I need her right now, and Tariq can miss me with that bullshit. I just want to be up under my sister right now, that's all. Let me shoot her a text and let her know I'll be there at eight thirty PM according to the pilot.

Kaniya: *I'm aware, your man called me.*

Killany: *What did he say???*

Kaniya: *If he wanted you to know he would've told you. Bye-bye, I'll see you later.*

Killany: *Really Kaniya??*

Chapter 11

Kaniya

Raven and I were headed to the airport to pick up Killany. I didn't feel like telling her what Yung said, I'll tell her face to face. I have enough problems going on in my life and texting back and forth with her isn't going to cut it. I know this is Killany's first real relationship. When Lucky and I first started out it was amazing. I gave that man six years of my life, I loved him with every breath in me. If I could change the past, I would do a lot of stuff different. I ignored a lot of shit when I should've been chin checking his ass. When the shit hit the fan the way it did, I walked away, I gave up and didn't fight for the shit that we built, now shit is all bad. I don't want that for Killany and Yung, take it from somebody that knows.

Don't get me wrong, I love Tariq, and I'm deeply in love with him too, but I was in love with Lucky; that man had my heart. The shit that I just found out about him crushed my soul, and I'm a strong woman that won't fold. That shit broke me, and those feelings that I have can never be thrown away. I don't regret anything that I've done, and God doesn't make any mistakes. I'm woman enough to accept a lot of shit.

"What's wrong Kaniya, what you thinking about, you're in deep thought?" Raven asked. Kaniya has something serious on her mind, she's still beautiful on the outside looking in, but she's masking some pain. I hope Tariq is still not up to his bullshit.

"I'm fine Raven, nothing to worry about trust me," I said. Raven is watching me like a hawk, she swears she knows me. I don't want to talk about my shit it's an ongoing situation.

"Kaniya, let me keep it real with you. You have always been there for me. I watch you have everybody's back and be everybody's shoulder to cry and lean on, let me be there for you. I know you're hurting I can see it. The hurt is coming through your pores." Raven divulged. I loved my sister to death, literally, when I tell you we ride, we die, and we cry together. Whatever is bothering her, I want to kill it because I feel her pain that's why I spoke on it. Her vibe is normally neutral and vibrant, and she's not herself today. She looks the part, but she's not herself. She just got engaged a week ago. She probably won't fucking say anything now since we are approaching the airport and Killany is about to get in. I'm still going to press the issue. I want to know what's going on.

"Damn, I can't hide it from Ray. One thing about it, I respect everything she just said, and I'll let her know what's going on. Sometimes holding stuff in isn't good for you." I thought to myself.

"Hey, yawl, about time yawl pulled up," Killany shouted.

What's wrong with you Kaniya? Hey Ray, what I miss?" Killany begged. Something is going on, and it doesn't feel right. I need some fucking answers.

"That's what I said Killany. Kaniya has something going on that she doesn't want to discuss, but I'm all ears because she's pregnant with my niece and nephew and stress isn't good at all." Raven admitted. I wanted to get to the bottom of this shit.

"Lucky has a baby on the way by Yirah, and she's almost seven months pregnant," I concluded. There I said it.

"So what, fuck him and focus on Tariq. Don't worry about that shit Kaniya." Killany ugh I'm so sick of Lucky and his shit.

"Let that go, sis, it's not worth the stress. Focus on you and Tariq and what yawl have, it's beautiful." Raven uttered. She needs to really let that go ugh.

Chapter 12

Kaniya

That's why I didn't want to say anything. It's deeper than what yawl think. Yawl missing the point. She's almost seven months pregnant which means he made this baby on me when we were together. They were fucking way before Mac's party. If my babies are his, Yirah's child will be older than mine, so that's why I'm thirty-eight hot. That's why I keep shit to myself and shit because they don't understand.

"Oh, I'm sorry sis why didn't you fucking tell me? Let that shit go that's more of the clarification to let you know he ain't shit and fuck him, marry Tariq and move on. God puts people in your life for a reason and a season. As soon as Tariq comes into your life all of this stuff starts to come out, he's your purpose and your future, focus on that." Killany suggested. Lucky is the dog of all dogs ugh.

"Kaniya, I'm sorry that you were holding that in. I can't imagine how you feel, I want to take the pain away. Would you like for me to push that bitch when I see her to make her lose her baby? I know for a fact that she knew that you were with Lucky, I can't stand a sideline hoe." Raven blurted. Yirah got my sister fucked up, I never liked her. I was only cordial with her for the sake of Tariq and Mac.

"Ray stop, it's cool. It feels better since I've gotten it out and off of my chest. I found out a week ago, and I had a break down at the house with Tariq, and he was livid. It was right after he proposed. I apologized to him, it just hurt so bad. I don't ever want the two of you to experience that pain. It was awful, my heart was aching for days, and it still is. I gave that man six years of my life for him to shit on me." I conceded. I started crying all over again, emotions and this pregnancy has me in my feelings like a bitch.

"Calm down sis, don't cry, you will upset the babies. Pull over so I can drive. Please let it go for the sake of the twins and your sanity. "Killany scolded. Love will break down the strongest bitch I know. I don't think I want that shit. Oh, Lord, she needs to stop crying and soak those fucking tears up. Tariq is calling now, and her Bluetooth automatically connects and answers the damn phone.

"Kaniya where are you and what's wrong baby are you ok?" Tariq bugged. I swore to God if she somewhere fucking with Lucky I was going to push that nigga's cap back.

"She's with us Tariq, the babies are kicking extra hard," Raven acknowledged. Damn he was nosey and crazy I can tell in his voice he was ready to go off.

"Tariq, I'm here for the week I need to borrow her I'm going through some things and I need my sister, so she will not be coming home tonight." Killany boasted. Now that shit is out the way.

"You can come stay out at the house with us Killany, it's cool." Tariq volunteered. Hell no she's not staying at her house for a week fuck that she can come to our house.

"No, Tariq it's not the same. I like to lay up under my sister and sleep in her bed, if I come to your house, I won't get to do that. She'll be laying up under you so no I'll pass." Killany added. The nerve of him ole kidnapping ass nigga.

"Killany where your man at? You can't come here calling shots and shit. I'm engaged, and I need to lay next to my wife and seeds every night. I'm not making no exemptions for your ass," Tariq stated. Hell no, I didn't give a fuck about none of that shit.

"Baby I'm good we were just picking Killany up from the airport. I'll be home in a few. I love you." I stated. Tariq isn't going to let me stay gone from home for a week.

"I love you too, bring your ass home now, not later. Killany I'll see you at the house. I love you Ray-Boogie." Tariq said. Kaniya knows I'm not going for that shit. I better not fall asleep, and she's not next to me we're not doing that anymore.

"Kaniya your husband is crazy I don't know if I want you with him either. I changed my mind. I already told him you weren't coming home, so he needs to accept that." Killany said. Tariq's old possessive ass, I love how he loves my sister. He's having K withdrawals and shit.

"Killany, what the hell is going on between you and Yung for you to be on a flight to Atlanta and not Virginia? Why do you want to lay up under me, you missed our birthday bitch? I need to be laid under my husband, and if I'm not home by a certain time trust me, he's coming over here to get my ass. We will never go a night without lying next to each other. Whatever you and Yung got going on fix it if it can be fixed, what the fuck did he do? Do I need to take a flight to Jersey?" I asked. Something serious had to happen for Killany to bring her ass here talking about she wants to pillow talk with me. Bitch, Tariq eats my pussy every night before he goes to bed and tonight will be no different, she better call Ma over here. If I'm not home by ten PM he'll be outside, trust me. He doesn't like me driving at night period. Let me text my momma and tell her to come and get daughter she's going through something.

Ma: *Killany and Yung beefing about something and she needs some advice.*

Kaniya: *And what you want me to do? I have a date tonight? She ain't gon' listen to me. Tell Tariq you'll see him in a few days, damn you ain't going nowhere and he ain't either. Tell your date to come and get his daughter.*

Ma: *my date doesn't have any kids thank you. call your daddy yourself and tell him and get off my line.*

"Well, that didn't work my momma think she's slick I know her and my dad are back messing around. I saw the text messages in his phone. It looks like I'm stuck. Tariq will not come over here, he wants me to sell my house, not. We were finally making it to my house. I wish Killany would confide in Raven, hell she needs to go over Kaitlyn's house and bother her, she'll be glad to have her." I thought to myself.

"What happened Killany? Cartier's nosey ass shot me a text to see if I knew anything. "Raven blurted. I hate being left out of the loop. Nobody tells me anything, but I'm never in any body's business.

Chapter 13

Killany

Wait until we make it to the house I'll tell you over food and wine. I know Kaniya doesn't want to be here but so what. All the times she was on my phone yapping about Lucky and whoever and laid in my bed pillow talking, return the favor. We were finally at Kaniya's house I didn't think that Raven would be here. I absolutely forgot that she moved in with Kaniya, so I guess I'll be telling her my business too. We have to bond because we are sisters too.

"Killany, I don't stay here, so I don't know if there's any food in the refrigerator or not. Mom moved back into her condo in Midtown, so it's just Raven here, we may have to order some food." Kaniya said. Shit, I don't even cook no more, Tariq does that too.

"That's fine, what do you guys want?" Killany asked because I definitely want some wings and pizza.

"Whatever you decide is fine." Raven agreed. I want some pizza.

"Pizza and wings." I decided. I'll place the order.

"Bitch let's get to it what happened," Kaniya mentioned. We need to get this show on the road it's almost ten PM, and I know Tariq will be hitting my line in a minute.

"Give me your phone Kaniya and yours too Raven I know how you like to record people and send shit to them. I don't want Cartier in my business. Kaniya I know Tariq will be calling soon. I'll answer your phone and tell him you are asleep." I advised. Kaniya can't fool me I know how she operates.

"Killany we are not doing that; I'll tell Tariq myself that I'm going to stay over here to be with you. I don't need you taking my phone and shit like I'm some little ass kid." Kaniya stated. This bitch done lost her damn mind.

"Killany you are crazy. "Raven laughed. She is on one, she's doing entirely too much.

"This is what happened; Yung and I were supposed to go house shopping today, and we ended up going to the warehouse. Remember Kaniya when I FaceTimed you there earlier, and Armony was with us? Well somebody tried to rob KC and Yung, I saw it on the surveillance system, so me and Armony suited up and went to work, leaving no faces and no future cases. He's mad about that shit, he was talking to me all reckless and shit. I didn't like it, so I left. To make matters worse, he has been going through my phone and erasing all of my text messages and shit. He didn't even try to stop me or nothing when I left. I looked through his phone two bitches were texting him and shit. It's too much I don't have time for his bipolar ass." I stated. I just put it out there. I can tell that Raven is shook just listening to this shit.

"Killany, so Yung is mad because you went to work not asking no questions? That's what the fuck you were supposed to do shit. I would've done the same. It's a pride issue trust me, powerful men can't stand women who are just as powerful. He didn't know that you could handle yourself in those type of situations. It's either killed or be killed." Kaniya said. I can't believe that's why he's tripping he needs to get over it.

"Wow, Killany you had a long day I'm sorry you had to endure that, but I'm here for you. He should've just been glad that you were there and was quick on your toes. Teach me how to be like yawl." Raven said. My sisters are fucking nuts I don't know who's worse, but I want to be the worst.

"It's in your blood Ray trust me," I stated. After she beat ole girl's ass in New Orleans, I knew she was my sister.

"Cartier sure did call me and asked me what was going on," Raven mentioned. I didn't tell him shit he knew something that I didn't and he didn't care to share.

"Killany do you love Yung? You never mentioned you guys getting a house together? Just fall back, I think it's pretty dope you had his back like that. Tell that nigga in the future don't take you around that shit if he's not ready for how you get it popping. So, you mean to tell me, Armony's cute ass was on go too?" Kaniya asked. Killany is sneaky as fuck; bitch ain't told me shit about her and Yung looking for a house together, must be serious. I hope that nigga knocks her feisty ass up.

"I do love Yung, am I in love with him, not yet. Yes, he wants us to get a house together. Fuck talking about Yung I want to go out tonight and show off. I want you guys to put me on Snapchat and Live. I want Yung to wonder what the fuck I'm doing you, feel me. Kaniya you're going too. I don't want to hear nothing about that pregnant shit. Just a few months ago, you were booed up with that nigga Dro until he let your ass go. Where's his fine ass at anyway?" I asked. I could tell

Kaniya was ready to bail, she's going to be my wingman.

"Bitch, you have some nerve coming here with all of this bullshit. Let me tell Tariq to come too then, and I'll record you on Live or Snapchat or whatever else you want. Don't say shit when Yung come's here on the first flight leaving from Jersey, you are on your own." Kaniya stated. I can't believe Killany's doing this get back shit, she's really feeling Yung. I see a lot of my mom in her now since she's dating. Let me call my mom.

"What Kaniya Nicole, what do you want little girl? Didn't I tell you I was on a date tonight?" Kaisha asked. I'm tired of her cockblocking ass.

"Who's that man in the background? Hey, daddy Killany's here," Kaniya asked. My momma thinks she slick, keep that shit real that you're back with your husband.

"Hey, Kaniya, Raven, and Killany! What are you guys up to on a Friday night? Killany why haven't you called me. I see that you're starting to act like Kaniya now too. When will I meet Yung, what's his real fucking name?" Killian asked. Kaisha wanted to be secretive about us dating again. I don't know why we are still married.

"Daddy, what are you doing with my momma? I have been calling you, you've just been ignoring me. You can meet Yung whenever you want too. I could never act like Kaniya, and you know it." I said. What's really going on, the two of them in the same space? What did I miss? Last I checked they couldn't stand each other. I was daddy's little girl now Raven and my momma, oh hell no.

"Hey, daddy I thought you were taking me on a date this Friday? You're playing me to the left for my momma. Come and get me now, I meant come and get us know," Raven joked. Those two think they're slick, but they're not. I already knew what time it was when he started coming by the house frequently like he was coming for me. He was really coming by to see if his wife was around. I'm glad they were back together.

"Let me be the first to tell you... click." Killian said. Kaisha why in the fuck did you hang up in their faces? I wish she'd grow up. I'm glad you have a close relationship with our daughters, but still, she needs to act forty-five and not twenty-five they'll still respect her the same. I see what Kanan is saying now.

Chapter 14

Kaisha

I don't want their nosey asses in my business, we can tell them another time, but not today. You can finish eating my pussy that's what you can do." Kaisha said. Kaniya better be glad that she's pregnant because I would put my foot up in her ass questioning me about what the fuck I'm doing. Killany and Raven too, I'll be by there tomorrow to chin check their asses.

"You want me to continue to suck and fuck you when you want me too, but you don't want to let our children know that we are back together? I don't understand you at all Kaisha, but let me find out you're still on your little single shit you used to do. I promise you I'll kill you and that nigga. You know what, fuck that I'm leaving, I'm nobody's side nigga. Let me go see my daughters since they want to see their daddy. You need to grow up." Killian said.

"I'm really going to fuck my children up now. I was just about to nut until they called and fucked shit up. I wasn't ready to tell them yet, so what. Kaniya's sneaky ass already knew somehow anyway. Killian was the love of my life, no man could ever compare to him. Let me call the girls up now and tell them because he was not about to leave up out of here because he wanted me to do some shit that I wanted to do on my own time. I made my way to the bathroom and put the phone on speaker so he could hear since he was in the shower anyway." I thought to myself.

"What ma why did you call back after you hung up in our face? I already knew what he was about to say. I just wanted to hear from his trap queen Kaisha with the K." Kaniya laughed.

"Kaniya Nicole, don't fucking play with me I'll bust your ass, pregnant or not, my grandbabies won't be able to save their momma. Yes, I'm back with my husband, do any of yawl have a fucking problem with it. Yawl nosey asses already knew that anyway. Yawl just wanted me to say the shit out of my own mouth. Stop calling my husband's phone after ten PM if yawl must know." I argued. There I said it.

"Ma, why didn't you tell me?" Killany asked.

"Killany, you know you talk too fucking much, let's be honest." Kaisha laughed. I wouldn't tell Killany shit if she was the last person on this earth. Kaisha thought to herself.

"No wonder you don't have time for me no more ma." Raven laughed.

"I'm happy for yawl, about damn time." Kaniya congratulated. Daddy can stay out of my business and tend to his wife's business.

"Cut the bullshit. I'll come by and see the three of you tomorrow." I laughed. What am I going to do with those three? I owe Kaniya and Raven one.

Chapter 15

Killany

Kaniya, leave Tariq's ass at home, damn let's just hang out tonight. Who knows when we will be able to do this shit again. I need the old Kaniya back if it's only for tonight. The bad bitch that doesn't give a fuck about nothing, who doesn't mind stepping on a bitch's toes. Where is my sister that's down to ride for me no matter what? The one who I was looking up to and was wishing I was in the mix with when all of her bullshit was hitting the fan. Remember I was the one you were calling. You flew to VA to see me, and you laid up in my bed for two weeks in your feelings about two niggas. I had to read Kaniya's ass. Bitch, please don't act like you're better than anybody because you have a rock on your finger. You were just on my line a month ago, heavy kicking it with that nigga Dro, telling me how much fun you were having. Now all of a sudden you and Tariq are back heavy and engaged, what the fuck did I miss. I like Tariq, but fuck him too.

I have to step in and say something. I could tell Kaniya was ready to lay hands on Killany. "Hey that's enough we are sisters, will we not be doing this shit. All this back and forth shit. I'll call Tariq my fucking self, and let him know that you won't be coming home tonight, or for as long as Killany needs you. He can't do nothing but respect it. Go get dressed I refuse to listen to you two anymore." Raven said.

"I'm glad Raven said something when she did because obviously, Killany had some shit on her chest that she had to get off and I was her prey. I'll take that, though because I was ready to box with Killany's ass, please don't get it confused because I'm pregnant, we can still get fucking to it. I'm surprised at Ray, I guess we are rubbing off on her she commanded attention when she spoke. Let me call Tariq and give him the business.

"Kaniya, are you on your way home?" Tariq asked.

"No, I'm not coming home I'm going out with Killany and Raven. Killany's going through some things, and she really needs me. I'm sure I'll be home tomorrow though she has some tricks up her sleeve and I'll bet you any amount of money that Yung will be here before the sun comes up." Kaniya stated. I know Tariq will understand hearing it from me.

"Oh ok Kaniya, don't make this shit no habit. You shouldn't be going to no club anyway, and you're pregnant with my seeds. Only for tonight, though. I'm hungry I can't even eat you, I'm going to starve tonight huh? Don't be wearing no tight ass shit either. Where are yawl going so I can pull up," Tariq asked. I needed to see my wife tonight. I respect everything she just said, and I'll let her do her thing with her sister's, but I still wanted to see her.

"I don't know where we are going, but I will text you as soon as we pull up. I love you, and I'm about to get dressed." Kaniya said. He's so understanding.

"I love you too, and I'll see you tonight," Tariq said. I had to see her, I don't give a fuck who's in town.

"I was ready to get out and let my hair down. I needed to apologize to Kaniya first I just straight went in on my sister, I have never done that before. Thank God Raven was there; I just knew we were about to fight. Kaniya, can I come in?" I asked.

"Sure, why not. "Kaniya said. I motioned with my hands for Killany to come in. Lord, please don't let Killany say anything out of the way to me. I promise you I'll forget that we shared the same womb.

"I'm sorry Kaniya I'm going through some stuff, and I don't know how to control these feelings. This relationship shit is new to me and the way Yung talked to me in front KC and Armony, that shit still fucks with me. He didn't have the decency to say what he had to say behind closed doors. "I said. I promise you I don't like feeling like this, but I can't shake the feeling. This shit is new to me, you should understand.

"I'm sorry too, and I should be there for you no matter what because you've always been here for me. I'm so sorry Killany, please forgive me, but get out your feelings bitch so we can show Yung how we do this shit. Let me dress you up and flat iron your hair so this nigga can really lose it, I'm the queen of petty. Let me beat your face too, he ain't fucking ready. Watch K work!" Kaniya yelled. Lord Killany has gotten my pregnant ass too piped up. I feel used, but if she wants to use my tactics be prepared for the heat that comes with it.

"Awe yawl made up? Good, glam me up too I want to break some necks." Raven said.

"Ok let me pick you out something to wear too. Damn why do I have to be pregnant, man you two are making me want to cut up and be petty." Kaniya said. Ain't this some shit these two heifers on some messy shit. I can't be involved fuck my life. I picked out Killany and Ray both some fly ass shit that I would wear to cut a fool. I think Onyx would be perfect for tonight, it's always plenty of eye candy in there and niggas with money. I was bringing two of the baddest ladies out tonight.

I made Killany put on a True Religion skirt and this cutout shirt that shows her stomach because she was toned. Oh and her hair and was bone straight and face beat, yeah that's all me. Oh, and let's not forget about Ray; Robin Jeans shorts and oh my they were short and the matching blue jean vest to match with no bra and a cute messy bun, face beat with some nice red lips and some nude Red Bottoms. Yung & Cartier will have some act right tonight. I'm Snap chatting everything.

"I finally had that old Kaniya back if only for one tonight. I came to Atlanta for a reason because I know my sister is always with it. I could've gone home to Virginia and called King, but I didn't want to do that. Yung would expect that from me, but this savage ass shit I'm about pull here, he wouldn't even see me coming with this. We were finally ready to go Kaniya was laughing the whole time she was feeling herself even though she couldn't get loose like me and Ray. She was down, she cut her phone off because Tariq wanted to see her. We loaded up in Kaniya's truck she had to be the DJ, she would play songs that you least expect like Trina the Baddest Bitch she loves Trina she swore Trina raised her and not Kaisha. We were going to Onyx tonight she picked the spot the GPS said we were arriving in about thirty minutes." I thought to myself.

"Yawl two are mighty quiet over there don't do nothing that I wouldn't do," Kaniya mentioned. This shit was hilarious; I can't believe

Killany right now, Yung has to be that nigga. She's getting ready to cut up. Damn, she looks just like my momma. Raven's so pretty it's ridiculous; Tariq and Sonja are going to kill me. I'm so mad I can't join in on the petty shit. If Yung is wild like I think he is, after this stunt he'll be here before Killany can lay her head on my pillow.

"Really Kaniya you know you're a hot ass mess, you can't stop smiling over there. You wish you could be on your single shit." Raven said. Kaniya loves to play games, I'm glad Tariq locked her ass down because she and Dro were kicking it pretty heavy.

I can look in Kaniya's eyes and tell she misses her little bullshit she used to do. She needs to makes sure that she wants to get married. "Kaniya, you miss this shit, don't you? "I asked.

"This night isn't about me it's about yawl, so let's have fun it's a celebration. Damn I'm mad I can't have a drink we're here now let's get this show on the road. "Kaniya thought. Let the games begin. Tariq just told me to stay off of social media.

"The line is super long," Raven stated. Damn, I don't feel like standing and waiting.

"Ray, we don't do lines baby, we valet park and we VIP everything, nothing more, nothing less," Kaniya stated.

Chapter 16

Killany

It's show time. I rubbed my hands together like Birdman. I knew Yung was about to blow a gasket. He doesn't do social media, but KC, Cartier, and Armony are on it, so I know his phone was about to be going off. Onyx was actually lit tonight, the line was extremely long and the cars in VIP were flashy as fuck. It's time to find some prey. As soon as my foot stepped inside of Onyx they were playing Watch Me Walk Through by Rich Homie Quan, that was my cue. I needed Kaniya to put me on live right now on both sites. My walk was extra mean tonight, and this skirt did my ass no justice. The DJ switched it up and played Dun Dun by Shawty Lo everybody went nuts. I had a bucket full of ones and threw at the strippers. R.I.P Shawty Lo.

"Sis, you got these folks going wild eight hundred people are watching between Facebook and Snapchat this shit lit Raven let me get you too" Kaniya chuckled. Killany and Raven are killing this shit right now. It's actually a good night, the dancers looked really good, and it was packed wall to wall. Money was being thrown from everywhere. I wonder if Ray and Killany want a lap dance.

"Let's get a VIP booth so we can really turn up, I heard Future was in the building," Raven yelled over the music.

"Hey there, let's get it," Kaniya quoted. The music has me in my zone. It's about to be a zoovie if Future's in the building. We made our way to the stage where the dancers were dancing. Killany and Ray had ones on deck blowing stupid cash, they were dancing and throwing money. The DJ played Future's Commas and Killany went nuts. Some guy walked up behind her and grabbed her, she threw that ass back. Of course, I had it on live. She looks like she was enjoying that shit. I guess Yung had seen enough because here goes that call interrupting the feed.

"I could see now this shit was going to end up all bad. I haven't looked at my phone all night. I had a missed text from Cartier talking about don't have too much fun tonight and get a nigga fucked up behind enjoying yourself too much. What the fuck was that supposed to mean. Last I checked he was single and so was I. I didn't have anything to do with what Killany and Yung had going on and neither did he. I was just enjoying myself with my sisters that's it. I did get ole boy's number. I was going to hit him up tomorrow. Cartier does him, why can't I do me." Raven I thought to myself.

"What's wrong Ray, what happened?" Kaniya asked. I don't know who just pissed in Raven's cheerios. Her aura changed all of sudden like she was thinking about some shit. I was having fun too. I didn't need the Debbie downers to show up, not tonight. They wanted me here to bring the heat don't switch up now.

"Nothing too much. Here look at this text message from Cartier." Raven stated. The nerve of him.

"Why is he mad, you two are not exclusive?" Kaniya asked. Yung and Cartier are crazy. I thought my life was complicated.

Chapter 17

Yung

Here I am at home tripping about how Killany just up and left a nigga. Cartier hit me up with his password and login for Facebook and Snapchat. I log in and see Killany. This doesn't even look like my bitch she looks brand new. No natural curly hair, she has hair bone straight looking like a video vixen. It was cool that she was flexing. I wasn't going to trip, but when I saw that nigga all in her ear and his hands on my hips. She was smiling like she was feeling whatever he was spitting. I was livid we are not doing this shit. I knew Kaniya had to be the one recording I could hear her ass laughing she made sure she zoomed in so I could see that shit. Raven looked different too. I called Killany's phone at least six times, and I kept getting cleared out.

I had access to a private jet, and that bitch could leave in the next thirty minutes. I'll be in Atlanta in two hours. I knew the club manager of Onyx; I made a call and let him know don't let my bitch leave the club, she thinks this shit is a game. I don't tolerate disrespect at all. See, Kaniya loves to play games I'm sure this was her idea. Killany got me fucked up she knows I'm savage ass nigga and I do savage ass shit. I already told her about conversing this man is about to die because he had hands on my bitch hips and she knows better. Let me call Cartier to see if he's riding out Kaniya's trying to turn Raven out too.

"Yeah, sucker." Cartier laughed I can see Yung's face now, I know he's thirty-eight hot.

"I'm catching a flight to Atlanta you coming." I asked Cartier. I can't even believe Killany would do some shit like this.

"Really Yung for what." Cartier laughed.

"To get my bitch and murk that nigga," I said. My voice was dripping with venom I know Cartier could tell.

"Yeah sucker, I'll ride out with your pussy whipped ass." Cartier laughed. Yung's crazy as fuck.

"You mad because you aren't getting none. Raven didn't look like she was a virgin tonight." I laughed. His silly ass didn't see the niggas that were up in her face.

"Kaniya's laugh infuriated me. I had something for her ass, though. I love to handle bold Bitches. Killany just straight disrespected me, and I have to show her I don't tolerate that shit at all. Our relationship will not be based off of no tit for tat bullshit. Kaniya should be ashamed of herself; pregnant and in the strip club with your sisters knowing damn well, Killany has a fucking man. I'm not a fuck nigga like Tariq and Lucky, my woman will not act as such. She wants to be like Kaniya so bad, but I'll show her tonight why in the fuck she doesn't want to be like Kaniya. Speaking of Kaniya let me shoot her a text.

Yung: *Play with your twins you don't want to play with a nigga like me behind my woman*

Kaniya: *You saying that, to say what?*

Yung: *You'll find out!*

Kaniya: Will I? I don't see you fuck nigga, reveal yourself. You better ask about me. Don't go off what you see and as far as your woman that's my fucking sister. If you got an issue you shouldn't have let her board a flight now reveal yourself.

"I don't like how Kaniya was talking to me, but that was all the clarification that I needed to know that Killany was on some bullshit. How we ended things earlier and shit it was all my fault. Two wrongs don't make a right, but that shit don't matter to me. The fact that she thought it was cool to just straight disrespect me. I don't tolerate disrespect at all." Yung thought to himself. I can't wait to get my hands on her. I have never done the shit that I'm about to do, but I have to let her know don't fuck with me because you in your feelings about a disagreement that we had. Killany wanted to be grown, but she wanted to be childish also. Just be prepared to play this shit how it goes. I'll go to war with whoever. It doesn't matter I don't give a fuck, loyalty and respect is all that matters to me. I would never act this way over a disagreement. She'll learn today just watch.

"Yung was dragging me to Atlanta just to fuck Killany up. I saw Raven's fine ass too; we were just dating, and I like Raven a whole lot we haven't put a title on what we were doing yet. I like the way she looked tonight. I could tell she was having fun. I didn't like her having it with a nigga that wasn't me." Cartier stated. She needs to let me put some dick in her life. I know she read my text, but I meant what I said. She knows that don't I tolerate disrespect. Whatever you do on your time is fine, but I don't need to see what the fuck you and another nigga is doing in my face. I'll see her in a few.

Chapter 18
Kaniya

I can't believe Yung shot me a text about some bullshit, he didn't scare me, though. I'm one bitch that a nigga can't scare easily. He said he'll be here in two hours. I'm not even going to tell Killany. I can't wait to see how this nigga coming and he better not half step, if he does I'll tell Killany that he's not worth it. Let me add some more fuel fire because I'm messy I want Yung on straight savage mode when he pulls up. Looks I'll be getting my pussy ate tonight. I'm so devilish.

"Damn Mrs. Shannon you looking mighty fine. I'm coming for you when it's my time and when you least expect. Take that ring off of your finger before I do it my damn self." Dro stated. I had to let my presence be known. I've been eye fucking her all night. Kaniya got me fucked up she knows I want her in the worst way. If I have to kill Lucky and Tariq to get her, that's what the fuck I'll do.

"Dro don't do that you in here with two bitches, and you've been eye fucking me all night. I haven't broken up your party with your bitches because I have respect for you." I said. He's too crazy I can't deal with him. Dro was a really good distraction. I was watching his ass all night too.

"Give me a hug. Let me taste it for old time sake?" Dro asked. She tastes so fucking good. Hands down she was the sexiest female that I've seen in a while, but I had to let her go.

"Um huh, we are definitely not doing that." I laughed. I

couldn't be that close to Dro without my legs being wrapped around his face. I hate that he is even here right now talking to me. Trust and believe, I would've taken him up on his offer, he's the head doctor.

"Sis, you good?" Killany asked. Who was this fine ass man that Kaniya was talking to that wasn't Tariq? I can tell that he had feelings for my sister, it was evident in his eyes. I could see it in her eyes that she was lusting.

"She's good but who are you? Kaniya you didn't tell me that you had a twin. I could've been with her instead of your confused self. I'm Dro, and you are?" Dro asked. Damn Kaniya's sister was fine as fuck. Kanan should've turned me on to her. It's too late now I fucked around and caught some feelings for her.

"I'm Killany it's nice to finally meet you, Dro, I've heard a lot about you. You're really handsome, Kaniya gets all of the good ones." Killany laughed. Damn, he's fine. She described him to the tee. He was real thuggish like she liked them.

"You can have me, what's up? Kaniya's getting married, but she didn't run that shit by me. So, what's good, you want to fuck with a nigga or what?" Dro asked. I had Kaniya hot with that comment. I wanted to know how she felt. She had some feelings for me that she didn't care to act on. I caught her watching me too.

"I would never do something like that to my sister, but I have a man, though. I appreciate the offer. It was nice meeting you, let's go Kaniya." Killany said. Kaniya must have fucked him or something, he's tripping over her. He's bold as fuck, he's going to be a problem for her in the future. I can't tell her hard head ass shit.

"I meant what I said Kaniya, when it's my time I'm coming for you shawty. Body's will be dropping, and it won't be mine, get your black dress ready." Dro yelled. I wanted that to stay on her mind. I was serious about that shit too. That's the only way I could have her if Lucky and Tariq weren't in the picture. It's like her juices were crack every time she fed me her pussy I was getting hooked, that's why I had to cut her off. I was nobody's side nigga, and I didn't want her to be my side bitch.

"Kaniya, what's up with him? What happened?" Killany asked. He's crazy as fuck. I've never seen nothing like it before.

"Nothing, we were friends. That's it. He likes to show out and shit. I'm not tripping off him. I put this good pussy in his mouth, that's it nothing more nothing less." I laughed. I liked Dro's crazy ass, I missed him too, that's why I wanted to come here I knew I would run into him.

"You need to stop that shit seriously." Killany laughed. She'll learn one day. I promise you she's always in some shit.

"I wasn't going to tell you, but Yung is on the way he should be here any minute now. That nigga is on go, so be ready. This is what you wanted, so be prepared. Let's go out with one last bang." I said. We made our way toward the stage where the strippers were. I was feeling myself, I started dancing. Dro was watching me from across the room our eyes always found each other.

The DJ started playing *Spend It* by Dae Dae. The shit was lit, Exotic was dancing, and some guy was blowing stupid cash. He had a big duffle bag full of money.

Spend that shit

Spend that shit

Spend that shit

Spend a check and get it right back

The strippers were going crazy; cash was being thrown from everywhere. It was a mess tonight, I had so much fun, though. Tariq sent me a text.

Hubby: *Why is that nigga up in your face?*

Wifey: *He was just speaking.*

Hubby: *That's not what the fuck it looked like. Bring your ass on now. I'm outside.*

"Killany, what's good?" Yung's voice boomed over the speakers in Onyx.

"Oh shit." I laughed. It's show motherfucking time.

"What's going on Kaniya and Killany?" Raven asked. They're crazy I can't be bothered with them. I knew it, something bad was about to happen. I could feel it.

"Just watch and see Killany wanted this shit. I wanted to see how Yung was coming." I said. I live for shit like this.

"What's good Yung?" Killany laughed. This nigga is heated. His face is all knotted up.

"Come here for a minute. Follow me, stay back Kaniya this ain't got shit to do with you. Cartier get Ray." Yung called. I motioned with my hands for her to come and see me.

"You good Killany?" I asked. Yung's calling the shots now.

"Yeah I'm great." Killany laughed. Oh, Lord, this shit is about to get real. Everybody is looking at us. I don't like this type of attention. Yung is the type of nigga that can't do simple shit, he's very extra.

"Killany, we are together, right? Sit right here." Yung yelled. This bitch had me livid. I handcuffed her to the chair and sat that nigga right by her whose hands was on her hips. She was looking at me crazy and shit. I wasn't going to kill her, but she made this man a target. She knew better and if she didn't know she would know today.

"What's going on Yung?" Killany asked. This motherfucker is crazy. He has lost his fucking mind.

"Have I ever disrespected you?" Yung I yelled at her. I was in her face now, she got me fucked up. I don't have time to play with Killany.

"No, not that I know of," Killany stated. What the fuck is he trying to prove?

"We had a small disagreement, and you wanted to do some spiteful shit, and you knew I would come here and act a fool. Do you know what the fuck I'm capable of? This man is about to lose his life because my bitch was being friendly and in her feelings. Again, never make permanent decisions on temporary emotions." Yung yelled. I made sure she understood what the fuck I meant because I was all up in her face. I grabbed my machete and chopped this fuck niggas hands off, and I threw his hands on her pretty ass. The look on his face. I took my Glock 40 and blew his fucking brains out. I threw his head on Killany, blood was everywhere. I made sure she was covered in his blood. It was her fault he died tonight, not mine. She was livid and crying. Don't fucking play with me bitch, I'm that nigga, and I'm jealous as fuck don't you ever fucking disrespect me.

"Really Yung you did all of this bullshit. Uncuff me now. It's over!" Killany cried. He took this shit too far what he just did was very disrespectful. I would never do anything like this to anybody.

"I'm not doing shit. You in your feelings huh? How do you think I felt when his hands were on something that was supposed to be mine? It's over? I'll kill you before I ever let you leave me." Yung yelled. She's mad now she wants to holler it's over now. She wasn't screaming that shit when she wanted a reaction.

"Yung, let me up in this bitch," I yelled. I was banging on the door. He got my sister fucked up. I heard Yung yelling at Killany like he was crazy.

"I don't know who Kaniya thought she was, but she has life all fucked up," Yung yelled. I opened the door with my Glock 40 pointed to her head and to my surprise she had her Glock 40 pointed at my head too ain't this a bitch. I grilled her, I didn't like her for some reason.

"Killany what the fuck you want to do? Do you love this nigga if not he's a done fucking deal? I'll squeeze this trigger so fucking fast, bitch say something? It's always you over him, give me the go." I asked. Damn Yung is crazy. I knew some shit was going down, but damn he did all of this. Killany was covered in blood.

"I love him Kaniya put that shit up," Killany yelled. She was about to take this shit too far.

"Why in the fuck are you crying I'm not putting shit up? Please tell me you're not tripping off this blood. I thought he would do more than this. I'm not impressed by far, but for real Yung this was litty. Killany, I brought you some change of clothes. I love you, Killany

Denise. I'll see you later, my husband's face is waiting on me fucking with you. I told you how this shit would end up. I wish you two nothing but the best. Yung, take it easy on her she's new to this love shit, but my offer still stands. I'll off you fucking with her. When you look at her, that's all me. It's nothing that I won't do for her." I stated. I had to put that shit out there. I tossed Killany the bag of clothes that I brought for her. I knew she would need it.

"It' s a shower in there, go shower and get dressed now," Yung yelled. She made me do all of this shit. I've killed for less. She hit me with them crocodile tears.

"I just got up and did as I was told, I didn't feel like arguing with him. I had fun, though. Kaniya is a fucking mess. I wonder where Ray went? Her and Cartier are so cute together." Killany I thought to myself.

"Get that smile up off your face," Yung warned. I had the cleaning crew on standby. I was waiting on Killany to shower so they can come in and do what they do. I can't believe I let her take me there, she asked for it. She shouldn't expect anything less from me. She could forget about staying in Atlanta we were on a flight to Virginia after this and she can think about what the fuck she did.

Chapter 19

Killany

I can't believe Yung acted the way he did. I love Yung I really do, more than I should actually. He went over the top with that shit. He did not have to throw those damn hands on me and ole boys head, he was doing too much. I took my time in the shower. I was covered in blood, and he messed my hair up.

"Killany hurry up, I know you are fucking finished," Yung yelled. She's taking her time on purpose. I can't be doing this shit.

"I cut the shower off I needed to deep condition my hair. I knew blood was still in it. I dried off; Kaniya set me up. I needed to look at what she put on Live because whatever Yung saw he was livid. I put on the clothes that Kaniya gave me which was a maxi dress, and this dress was tight and little as fuck. It stopped at my thighs, my ass was playing peek a boo. She wanted me to die today. I just knew Yung was going to flip. I was scared to walk out the bathroom. I could beat Kaniya's ass right now; that's one childish ass motherfucker." I thought to myself. I had to pray on my way up out of here. God forgive me for all of my sins, tell my daddy I love him.

"Killany, what the fuck is this? Come here you want me to put my hands on you, don't you? You never dress like this what's going on with you? Be yourself ma, you want attention? I can give you plenty of that, please don't ever disrespect me. Bend over let me inspect you. No panties really." Yung questioned. I smacked Killany on her ass hard as fuck. She should never disobey daddy. She is going to be the death of me. Damn her pussy looked right from the back. I had a car parked in the back, I was taking her home. I gave her my shirt to put on and ushered her to the car that was waiting for us.

"Let me give you Kaniya's address, so you can take me over there," I stated. I was scared to be alone with Yung right now. He just smacked me on my ass so hard. It's still hurting.

"Do you think I actually came here to take you back to your sister's house? You're riding and flying with me where ever I go." Yung asked. I had to let her know. I don't have time to be playing with Killany, she proved her point, and I proved mine.

"Why did you let me leave earlier Yung if you knew you were going to come out here?" I asked. I don't understand him at all.

"I didn't let you leave, you left on your own because you were pissed. I wouldn't have came here if you weren't doing some shit you had no fucking business doing. I thought you were better than that. I thought you were a lady, but I guess I was wrong. You still want to act like a little ass girl. I chose you for a reason, please don't make me regret that shit. Did I choose the right one?" Yung asked. I threw that out there because I saw a lot in Killany that she didn't see in herself. I haven't introduced her to mom yet, but I wanted too I felt like we could get to that point.

"You made the right choice Yung, and I apologize if I offended you or disrespected you in any way, but I didn't intend to do that. If we are going to do us and be one watch how you talk to me in front people. I don't appreciate how you talked to me in front of KC and Armony the way you did it was disrespectful. I would never do that to you." I stated. I had to get that off of my chest. He needs to learn to talk me like I'm his lady and not his child.

"KC and Armony are family. I need you and Armony to bond because if we are planning on living together. I might be gone days at a time, and I don't want you running around Jersey alone, and she's my right hand's girl. You get the picture? She's cool," Yung stated. I needed Killany to work on that for me.

"I hear what you are saying, but do you hear what I am saying? You have to apologize to me for how you talked to me "I stated. This shit works both ways, he can't even admit that he was wrong.

"Come here I want you to sit on my lap," Yung asked. I motioned with my hands for Killany to come over towards me. I could see where this conversation was going.

"Yung, thought he was slick, he thought that he didn't need to apologize, but he did. "I'll keep my thoughts to myself.

"I bit my teeth down on Killany's shoulders. I wrapped my arms around her waist and I sunk my teeth into her neck, and I licked her earlobe. I whispered in her ear I love you, and I'm sorry. Do you forgive me, keep riding for your man?" Yung revealed. I don't need Killany telling me what to do. I knew I had turned her on, her pussy was wet, and I could feel it through my jeans. Damn, I don't think I ever told a female I loved her before, this is definitely a first for me.

"I love you too," I admitted. That's a first. I could fuck Yung right here, right now. We finally arrived at the airport.

"Act like it." Yung declared. I know she wanted me to fuck her, but I'll pass I'm still pissed.

"Where are we going, Yung?" I asked. I noticed we pulled up to the airport.

"Virginia Beach, VA is that a problem?" Yung asked. Killany was about to be mad at me. I was taking her ass home, and I was going back to Jersey. I have some business to handle she'll be pissed some more. I was going to bless her with some deep stroke and dope dick, but her ass is on punishment.

"Virginia why not Jersey?" I protested. I'm confused did I miss something. Yung is up to something. I'll figure out exactly what it is, I'll roll with the punches for right now.

Yung

Our plane finally took off. Killany fell asleep on the flight. I couldn't stop looking at her she was beautiful, but she had some growing to do. I've been sitting back thinking about the shit that just transpired these past twenty-four hours. I could give Killany a great life. I have a lot to offer, and she does too. I wanted her to be herself and not somebody else. Hands down she was wifey. If we have an argument, don't run away and do spiteful shit because you wouldn't want me to do it. I used to be a dog ass nigga, but it's too many hoes out here that are dying to trap a nigga like me. I moved differently when it comes to choosing females. Our flight was landing now. I had a car waiting to pick us up. Wake up we are here.

"That was quick how long was I sleep?" I asked. I knew I was tired, I haven't had any sleep since this morning. I couldn't wait to get in my bed, it's been a long time coming. I haven't been home in over a month.

"Long enough to have slobber running down your cheek. "Yung laughed. She must have been really tired; her whole cheek is covered with slobber.

"Whatever don't look at me!" I shouted. I couldn't believe I was slobbering. I was having a dream, and it was getting good too.

"I don't care about that slobber on your cheek. I want you regardless. Come on and get off of here a car is waiting for us already." Yung mentioned.

Chapter 20

Armony

KC and I made it to New York yesterday about eight PM, we had dinner and went back to the room and just cuddled and looked at some movies. We were going to shop today. I checked my Snapchat, and Facebook and Killany was on this bitch lit. I hope and pray Yung didn't see this shit he would go nuts she wouldn't live to tell about it. Shit they were having fun I wish I was invited for the little turn-up. I was about to say something, but KC has signaled me to be quiet. He ordered us breakfast, and it looked amazing. I needed to talk to Killany Asap I shot her text, and I didn't get a response.

"Yo, Armony, I was talking to Yung that's why I didn't want you to say shit. Listen Killany went to Atlanta to cut up with her sisters Ray, K, and that shit was on Snap, Facebook Cartier messy ass got that shit started, and he caught a flight and a body. She served his ass good, though, he should've never let her board a flight to Atlanta anyway. Nobody wants their woman to be doing hot shit. I felt like she did what she was supposed to." KC said. He was being honest.

"I feel what you're saying. Is she ok, Yung didn't go too hard on her, did he?" I asked. I can't believe Yung went to Atlanta and showed his ass.

I know Killany, and I are not the best of friends, but I needed details on this shit that I know KC will not give me. Killany needs to face it we have to become really good friends for the sake of those two. I can only imagine how Yung cut the fuck up.

"Yeah she's ok he took her ass back to Virginia and he went back to Jersey." My man's Yung was too wild. I can't believe shorty's sister is buck like that.

"What's funny KC? I want to laugh too. "I said. KC thinks he's slick, he's leaving out something.

"Nothing, enjoy your breakfast. You and Killany need to bond some more because she should be comfortable enough to tell you what Yung just told me. The two of you just teamed up and caught a couple of bodies just yesterday without a care in the world on straight go mode." KC laughed. I had to give it to Armony she wanted to know what happened, but I don't tell Yung's business to nobody. If Killany wanted her to know, she would call and tell her.

Killany: *Hey, I'm good thanks for checking on me. Yung ran his mouth huh?*

"Babe she shot me a text back maybe we are getting somewhere." I laughed. Everybody needs somebody to talk too. I'm mad I wasn't there they looked like they were having mad fun. Menya's boring ass doesn't like to do shit like that.

Armony: *Actually no, I just saw the video on Snap and it was lit and KC said Yung went to Atlanta; he doesn't discuss Yung's business with me. I'm mad I wasn't there, that shit looked fun as hell. That little ass skirt got you fucked up, huh?*

Killany: *Oh yes, I had so much fun I don't regret any of it. It's been a while since I let my hair down. I had to beg my sister to come out to get it popping even though she's pregnant. She came out anyway and my youngest sister she came out too, but yes Yung showed up and out in the worst way. He dragged my ass back to VA only for him to leave right after. I can't deal with him. Enjoy your trip with KC I'll see you soon, hopefully.*

"Armony what do you want to do today? Baby, it's all about you tell me something. I feel a storm coming, and right now you're the only thing that seems real to me." KC asked. That was the God's honest truth. As long as I've been hustling and doing other shit what happened yesterday has never happened to me, but I was glad Armony was there, she was riding for a nigga no matter what. For some reason, I've been thinking about my mom heavy lately. I don't know why though maybe that's why I thought a storm was coming.

"Babe, we can weather any storm, what do you need me to do? I got your back forever. Who and what is fucking with KC? I will solve that shit, seriously, what you want to do Boss, let me get on my savage shit." I laughed. I was dead serious, it was time for me to be in the streets neck and neck with whoever. I wanted to be side by side with KC.

"Chill out Armony you're my secret weapon. I don't need everybody to know what you're capable of. If something was to happen to you, I wouldn't be able to live with myself. I love you more than you will ever know. Some things you don't want people to see. If I ever get jammed up, and I need some issues and situations handled that's where you come in at. A nigga wouldn't even see you coming.

Who would think your sexy ass would be a killer in disguise. I want to keep it that way.

Enough of that what do you want to do today. It's not often that we get away just the two of us," KC stated. Armony definitely had my heart, that shit belonged to her, every beat.

"The first thing that I want to do is make some fucking babies, next, of course, Time Square. You know I'm hotter than the street lights, so my feet need to tap the pavement. Third, dinner, of course, I'll let you choose. Fourth, it doesn't matter what we do as long as I'm with you." I stated. I really don't even feel like shopping, that's a first. I just want to lay up under KC we never really have time for ourselves anymore.

"Armony, you're ready to have my kids? Stop playing games I've been ready to knock your ass up. You're coming to New York, and you don't want to shop, I can't believe that. That's a first for Armony?" KC asked. I've wanted her to have my shorties for the longest, but I didn't want to pressure her. I felt like she would let me know when she was ready.

Chapter 21

Armony

I was glad that Killany hit me up. I really did want to get to know her. I'm glad that she was ok. Yung must be really feeling her to act out the way he did. Ugh, I think I put my foot in my mouth. I was ready to give KC some babies BUT not right now. My dad would go crazy if I had a baby and I wasn't married. He was so traditional and my mom too. If it happened, it happened, I would accept it. Tyler Perry's new movie Madea's Halloween was out, and I wanted to go see that, I ordered our tickets online. It's been a while since KC and I have done normal shit. I wanted today to be that day where we could just focus on us. I love to shop, but that shit didn't matter today he buys me shit all the time so I would ease up on his black card. I just wanted to be in the presence of my man. I wanted him to just hold me that's all, sometimes I just want to be held nothing more nothing less. I was listening to everything KC said earlier about a storm coming. I knew we could weather that. It was something else going on that he didn't care to share. When the timing was right, I was ready to hear it, and I was down to ride.

I needed to get dressed KC, and I have been lying around all day fucking like rabbits. If I wanted to have a baby anytime soon I'm sure we made one today, he couldn't keep his hands up off of me and his dick etched a permanent spot inside of me. We had reservations for dinner and a movie tonight. I couldn't decide on what I wanted to wear tonight. I guess I was going to dress up in a skirt and blouse, it was actually nice out.

I wanted to look good for my man so maybe some leather pants and my black leather bra and my leather jacket with my black Red Bottoms Lady Peep Spike Pumps. Yes, and when we were finished, he could rip these pants up off of me. Just the thought of that made me want to hurry up and get in the shower so we could get this date over with.

"Armony, let me get in with you really quick," KC asked. I was so happy that she was ready to have my kids I didn't want to ease up out that pussy. She would be pregnant before the month was out.

"No, because if you get in we'll have sex again and we won't make it to the movies and dinner," I shouted. I knew exactly what he was trying to do. It wasn't going to work this time. He was acting like a nympho, he knew I wasn't going anywhere.

"Oh really? I won't touch you if you don't want to be touched." KC yelled. Armony belongs to me, I get what I want, when I want it, wherever I want it. I got in the shower and grabbed the washcloth and made sure it was real soapy; I raised the shower head up some. I tapped Armony on her shoulder, and she turned around to face me. I could tell she had an attitude. I started washing her up from her head to her toes. I was finger fucking her. I knew her breast were her sensitive spot. I sucked them extra hard, and they became extremely hard. My tongue slithered and traced her stomach real smooth and stopped at her clit, and I attacked that fat motherfucker; she was hollering for me to stop and her legs began to shake. I knew she was about to cum. I had to grab her hips and her ass to stop her from falling, at this point, she was begging me to stop. I wouldn't let up though because she shouldn't have denied me anyway. I shoved my dick inside of her and started beating it out of the frame.

I pulled out and slammed it back in. Armony was small to me, I picked her up and turned her around I needed to beat that pussy up from the back now.

"KC, stop please I've had enough." I pleaded. He knew he was doing too much because I told him no. The water was fucking cold now. Ask me did he give a fuck.

"I'll ease up on you for now, but please don't ever deny me. Get dressed and make it extra sexy." KC said. I knew I pissed Armony off with that shit, but she'll get over it. Armony could have an attitude all she wants I don't give a fuck. She better be ready within ten minutes so we can leave. I don't have time for the attitude, she shouldn't have spoken on some shit that she wasn't ready for, the damage was already done now.

"I'm ready," I yelled. I can't believe him right now. He knew he was doing too much.

"Lose the attitude man if you feel that way, and if you do end up pregnant, I'll get you an abortion since you feel some type of way," KC yelled. She doesn't have to have my baby. She was the one that said she was ready, not me. I'm good I hated I started practicing today.

"Really KC, that's how you fucking feel it's not about being pregnant. You don't have to pay for me to do shit," I yelled. I can't believe he would fix his mouth to say some slick ass shit like that to me. I left his ass, I made my way to the elevator. I'll meet his disrespectful ass in the lobby before I say some shit that I'll regret.

"Oh, she fucking left I don't know what's her fucking problem. I'm not beat for this shit." KC yelled. She better be in the fucking lobby. I'm not with this extra shit. I made my way to the lobby she was buried in her fucking phone of course. I approached her and snatched her phone out of her hand.

"I don't know what's wrong with KC we were just fine less than an hour ago, when he had me bent over in the shower." I thought to myself. I just followed him to the car he was being real disrespectful and arrogant. The bastard didn't even open the door up for me. If he keeps it up, I'll check his ass.

"You good, you seem tense, and your attitude is dripping off you. Can you lose that shit so we can enjoy our night?" KC asked. I'm not feeling this shit at all. I hit the push to start on my Challenger the engine made a funny noise. I used the key this time it still didn't crank. I got out and checked the hood and soon as looked at engine two niggas ran up on me and insisted that I drop everything. Damn, I'm fucked. I got caught slipping.

"Drop that shit, pussy. Give me the keys and the cash," Khadafi yelled. I needed to make this shit quick. It was too many people looking.

"What the fuck is taking him so long? "I thought to myself. I'm ready to fucking go. The car was running just fine. I don't know what happened all of sudden.

"Pussy ass nigga make this shit easy for me. So, I don't have to slump you, give me your fucking keys and the fucking cash, and I'll let you go," Wesley yelled. This shit is taking longer than I expected.

"Is he getting robbed oh hell no I can't see shit. The hood is blocking my view, and the windows are tinted. It's gloomy outside because of the rain. I hope he has some guns in here. Damn I couldn't actually see how they had him cornered. I can't let him die damn. I found two guns I placed one behind my back and the other one in my pocket. I have to do this right because one wrong move and it's over for both of us. Here are the keys and here's some cash." I yelled. These two are so fucking dumb. It's like taking candy from a baby.

"You're a good bitch give it here," Khadafi stated. Damn she was fine and to make it even better she didn't want no smoke.

As soon as they approached me, I let this Glock 40 rip and dropped both of them niggas. One was still breathing. I killed one and shot the other one in both of his knees. KC put his foot on his neck. I can't believe all of this shit just transpired. I was ready to relax and enjoy our night. I was going to apologize to KC also. I was ready to have his babies. Here we were again in some more bullshit less than twenty-four hours ago. I just bodied three niggas, and it's the same shit today what the fuck is going on. I left one alive so we can get some fucking answers. Somebody was trying to get at KC bad, no matter the circumstances, and he needed to find out who it was because I was ready to close up my shop and ride passenger with him for the sake of my sanity. The past twenty-four hours I've been at the right place at the right time.

"Get in the car baby, thank you, I got it from here," KC advised. Something is going on I need to hit Yung up Asap. I couldn't even send this pussy to his maker because we were in New York and it was so many people looking, and shit and the police were on the way. Nobody knew I was coming to New York. These niggas weren't ordinary robbers the car alone cost more than what's in my pocket. I don't carry cash on me, I always let Armony keep the cash because they wouldn't expect her to have it. These niggas were sent here for me, they fucked up my car where it wouldn't start and attempted to rob me. I didn't even get the chance to ask who sent them. Armony played them so well like she was about to give everything up and dropped them niggas, quick.

KC: *Rock a bye baby two.*

Yung: *Location? I'm on my way.*

I knew a storm was coming, I felt it. The police finally arrived. Yung was on his way no questions asked. I needed to get back to my city ASAP. I needed to stay here. Also, my dad, has some connects here. I need to holla at ole boy that was still breathing to get a name. They took our statements. Armony was licensed to carry so it worked out in our favor. It was a lot of witnesses out so they waited and gave a statement. I brought Armony up here to get away not catch some bodies. The police asked did we want to file a police report and press charges, I declined since I knew he wouldn't live past tomorrow.

Chapter 22

Yung

KC hit my jack and told me some shit went down in New York, I was back on a flight to see what was good. What the fuck is really going on? I can't even close my eyes without shit happening, yesterday some shit jumped off at the warehouse and to make matters worse, everybody acted nonchalant about the shit. Nobody was paying attention, but Armony and Killany and they're not on my fucking payroll. I went to Atlanta to handle Killany's petty ass, she had to find out the hard way about playing with a nigga like me. I'm headed to New York, the only good thing about that is the flight isn't that long. I was about to land in about fifteen minutes anyway, at a private airstrip near JFK.

I tried to reach Killany she has my number on block I guess she's in her feelings about last night, I'll give her that, though. I'll see her soon if I can't get in touch with her. I'll be at her front door. Damn I need some sleep bad. I signed up for this shit, so I can't complain. KC needed me, and I was on my way. Armony caught another body. We need to get to the bottom of this shit. We didn't have any static with anybody that's why I was confused. We've been running things side by side for the past four years, and we've never endured anything like this. All of a sudden shit is happening every day. Somebody's plotting on us from the inside. It's time to switch shit up.

Armony

KC, are you ok? You haven't said shit since we got back to the room. What's the plan? What do you need me to do?

"I'm good are you ok? I hate that we have to cut our trip short and shit, You and I really needed some time alone. These past two days isn't a fucking coincidence, on the strength that you was with me and a nigga thought it was cool to get at me while my back was turned. I wasn't having that shit at all, I haven't made any noise in a while, I was trying to move different. I hope motherfuckers don't think that I've went soft because all of this poking at me and getting at me with indirect beef and I don't know anything about it. They were about to get a rude awakening, they should've prayed they killed me because I was coming, folks that I had beef with years ago families was about to come up missing because I need to make a statement it's not solving shit for them or me," KC yelled.

"Calm down baby we'll solve this shit," I stated. I pray whoever it is behind this runs for the fucking border, because once you come for KC, he won't let up. He will wipe out your whole family, he has honestly calmed down, and I loved it, he would give you hell for no reason, but now all of that is about to change. The streets ain't safe.

"Get the door and see if that's Yung," KC yelled. Yung is my charge partner; we mob together on whatever. I was sending Armony back to Jersey. I had some beef in this city, and I didn't need her with me. I didn't call Cartier because if we got jammed, I need him to be able to run shit, he didn't mob too tough with us, and that was the reason.

"Yeah, that's him. Come on in Yung. Why you do my girl like that?" I laughed. Yung looking all serious and shit, his loyalty to KC is so fucking bona fide. It doesn't make no sense; he never asks fucking questions. He rolled in with a big ass suitcase, I bet that bitch has a shitload of guns inside.

"That's your girl now? I didn't do nothing much but be me." Yung laughed.

"You brought everything? You ready to mob?" KC asked. I could look at Yung and tell he was on go, sleep didn't even matter right now.

"KC, don't insult me. Let's get this show on the road." Yung stated. KC knows I'm mobbing no matter what and I made sure I brought everything we needed before I took off.

"Armony it's some serious issues that I need to handle. I want you to catch a flight back to Jersey, and I'll see you tomorrow if not Sunday." KC pleaded. Armony's hard headed she'll fuck around and stay so she can mob with me.

"Really, KC why can't I stay? I want to mob with you too. "I asked. I can't even be mad at him. He wanted his right man with him.

"Baby, you've done enough already, but let me handle this shit ok. It's about to get messy, and I don't want you anywhere near this shit." KC stated.

"Yung what's Killany's address I'm going to VA to barge in? Is that cool KC that I go out there with her for a few days?" I asked. This bitch better not be with the shit and act like she's not at home.

"That's cool you can do that, Yung shoot her Killany's address, and I'll have a driver take you to JFK,"KC stated. Armony must be really feeling Killany's vibe, I'm glad it should be her over Menya any day. It's funny I remember when they first met they were about to go toe to toe in New Orleans.

Chapter 23

Armony

I don't know what I was thinking when I decided that I wanted to come to Virginia like Killany was my best friend. I just felt so connected to her for some reason, that shit is weird right. I observed the scenery, Virginia was a beautiful place. My flight just landed. My driver was due to arrive any minute now. I was nervous, this bitch better not be with the shit. I thought we got past whatever when we were in New Orleans and our little encounter the other day. I still haven't heard from Menya I wasn't losing any sleep, though. I didn't see what people saw in Menya that was my girl, though. I missed her I hate that shit went down the way it did. My driver pulled up, I was now headed to Killany's house. I said a quick prayer for KC and Yung and of course myself. The drive was actually pretty quick. Killany actually lived in a nice neighborhood, it looks snobby like her attitude. Let me stop I'm a visitor, and I hope she welcomes me. I made my way to her door, I rang her doorbell.

"Who is it?" Killany yelled. I wasn't expecting anyone, so I was curious to know why my door bell was ringing like a child was playing on my shit.

"I just stood there and didn't say anything. I rang the doorbell again. I rang it numerous times," I laughed. Killany was cussing her ass off.

"Oh, you think this shit is a fucking game. Who was playing at my fucking door at eight in the fucking morning? I swung my door open, I held my nine millimeter in my hand ready to blast a bitch and guess who it is Armony, I still had my gun trained in her face. What are you doing here? Why are you playing games?" Killany asked. This is strange, what is Armony doing at my house.

"Damn can I come in?" I asked. This shit can go left really quick.

"Sure, you can come in. Hold up, you got bags too?" Killany asked. Oh hell no. What the fuck did she think this is? You cool, but not that damn cool.

"Yes, I brought some fucking bags. I'm staying at your house for a few days. Is that a fucking problem? Yung and KC handling some shit right now. I couldn't join them, so I decided to join you," I stated. She was doing too much; this is why I didn't like her at first.

"Yeah, it's a fucking problem, I could've had my other boo here and you popping up and shit. Your nosy self shot me a text the other day. You decided to pop up today," Killany stated. I don't know who Armony thought she was talking to.

"You got a boo on the side? Bitch please, Yung will kill you before you can catch your fucking breath. I'm not here to debate with you show me where my fucking room is so I can unpack. Cook me some breakfast, and we can talk over food and coffee. Where's your hospitality? Whether you like or not, you and I have to be on one accord, it may take some time, but if you fucking with Yung for the long haul I'm going to be in the picture. I know for sure KC ain't replacing me. What about you are you replaceable?" I stated. I was

117

keeping it real. I know can't no bitch compare to me when it comes to KC, not even his mammy whoever that bitch is.

"You know what I'm not even about to go back and forth with you about nothing. The guest room is upstairs on the left. I'm flattered that you're infatuated with me, and you wanted to come and visit me. What would you like for breakfast?" Killany asked. Armony thinks she is slick popping off at the mouth talking about are you're replaceable, bitch I'm not looking to be kept by nobody, not even Yung.

"See that's wasn't bad you're a good bitch that MIGHT not be replaceable as long as you're fucking with me." I laughed. Killany is a mess. I'm starting to love her.

"I'm sure you told Menya that same fucking weak ass game about Cartier, look where it got her a hot pussy and broken heart. You know I'm that bitch that's why you are here. I put this grade A pussy on him, an irreplaceable mouth on him, and hummed like a hummingbird on that dick and he's been hooked ever since. I'm not in the business of keeping a man that doesn't want to be kept. If I'm not happy with Yung, I won't stay, I'll leave. That's the difference between you and me, Yung is replaceable too. I know my worth trust me I'm an asset in this relationship, not a liability. I bring a lot to the table." Killany declared... I'm a smart bitch. You can't tell me anything, and I believe it. I've sold a lot dreams to niggas too. I take this shit one day at a time.

"I didn't mean to ruffle your feathers, Killany. I just wanted to get you in formation," I vocalized. I'm just saying.

"Yo you messy as shit literally, I should've kicked your ass in New Orleans so you would know not to fuck with me," Killany yelled.

At least I busted her in her shit, she knows I don't play.

"You should've, BUT you didn't and what would make you think that you could kick my ass and succeed? Do you think I'm a weak bitch? Trust me I walk it like I fucking talk it, please don't judge me, I dare you to try me." I stated. Two alpha females with very strong personalities Lord make this work.

"Armony, I'm sorry. Let me stop because you and I will go back and forth all day and eventually we'll end up fighting. This is my home, and you're a guest, and I should treat you as such. If this is going to work, we have to start over. You are headstrong, and I am too, nothing can change that, I know you're not weak, but this ain't the time and definitely not at my place. Go upstairs and get situated. I'm going to cook breakfast, and we can get reacquainted and find us something to do." Killany said. I had to nip this in the bud because I could see where this was leading and I didn't want to provoke this bitch, all she wanted to do was get to know me, and I was open to that. We could be friends as long as she doesn't show me why we can't.

"You have a very nice place by the way," I stated. She had great taste. I love the décor it screams boss.

Chapter 24

KC

I have to call Armony to make sure that she made it safe. She's crazy, and Killany is crazy, and I don't want the two of them to kill each other. When I think about how they met and how they interact, it's the same way Yung and I met in middle school and shit. I was new to the school, we just moved to Jersey from California, you know everybody wants to pick on the new kid. My dad moved around a lot so my first day at the school I was taller than everybody, so these guys wanted to jump me, I'll never forget it as long as I live. I was standing at my locker and this one dude, Andre slammed the locker into my face, it was on from there. I had a reflex and rocked his ass to sleep, his crew tried to jump me it was three of them. Yung must have walked past and saw me fighting, he jumped in and started helping me fight. We've been partners ever since, but it wasn't easy. After he helped me, he brushed me off like he didn't want to fuck with me. The same way Killany acts with Armony, that's why it's funny to me.

Let me call her, though.

"Hey baby you miss me already, I miss you, I love you KC," Armony cooed into the phone.

"Hell yeah, I miss you, baby! I wish I could kiss you and bend that ass over, let me stop before I come out there and get you," I laughed. I miss her already.

"Awe make me catch a flight so we can baptize each other."
Armony laughed.

"Look at your hot ass. Where's Killany yawl haven't killed each
other yet?" I asked. Yung wanted to know she has him on block.

"Hell yeah, I was going to beat her ass in her own house. She
pulled a gun out on me and everything, Tell Yung he has a nut on his
hands. We're good now she's cooking breakfast, and I'm in my room."
Armony laughed. It was hilarious, I wish I would've recorded Killany,
her cheeks were red.

"Yo Armony, are you fucking serious right now, put Killany's
ass on the fucking phone.

"What the fuck did she do?" Yung yelled.

"Calm down both of yawl, we are cool now. Yawl do what the
fuck yawl need to do, and we are going to do us ok," Armony said.
God, they were tripping. I was ready to hang up.

"I hear you, but why in the fuck did she pull a gun out on
you?" I asked. I'm sick of Killany's rude ass. Yung better check her,
before I do.

"I was ringing her doorbell, and when she would ask who it
was, I wouldn't say anything, so you know the rest," Armony laughed.
It was really fun.

"There you go being messy, you need to cut it out," I stated.
She left that shit out.

"Where's Killany at now since she's not answering my calls?"
Yung yelled?

"She's cooking breakfast?" Armony said. Yung is crazy too,
that's what he gets.

"Put her on the phone," Yung asked. Killany got me fucked up because she's in her feelings at least I put her to sleep. I missed her, though. I wanted to hear her voice.

"Hold on, Yung. Killany come here. Telephone," Armony yelled. Pussy whipped ass. "Who is it? Your breakfast is ready, let's eat. "Killany asked. I don't have time for Armony's games.

"Just answer it and see bestie. "Armony laughed. I stuck my tongue out at Killany, she knew who it was.

"Hello, who is this?" Killany asked. I was irritated I knew it was Yung.

"You blocked my number?" Yung asked. Killany like to play mind games that's why I had to mind fuck her the other night. I'm in control.

"I did block you. You knew that of course. How can I help you? Did you leave something at my house?" Killany asked. Why did he ask a question that he already knew the answer to, just for me to clarify that shit?

"I did leave something at your house, I left you and your fucking whack ass attitude there. On some real shit unblock me, quit hiding behind that block button before I suffocate you in your sleep. Do you hear me?" Yung yelled. I swear she knows how to piss me off.

"I love you to Yung. I'm not unblocking you yet. I'll teach you how to love me soon bye." Killany I was not about to be on Armony's phone all day with Yung.

Killany

Yung is so crazy. I don't know what to say about him, but what I do know is that I'm not unblocking him. I fixed breakfast which consisted of waffles, omelets, grits, fresh fruit, fried tilapia.

"You cooked all of this for me. "Armony asked. Killany threw down. I have to send KC a picture of this.

"I cooked this for us. Why didn't you say that Yung was on the phone? You knew I wouldn't have came. He was wrong how he left my house without even saying anything." I asked. Armony was messy too, you wouldn't think so, but she is.

"I was talking to KC, and he was yelling in the background asking for you. I thought it was cute. I've never seen him act this way before," Armony stated. Yung was falling for Killany hard. He could deny it all he wants, but I knew the truth.

"So, what happened, Yung was just in Jersey now he's in NY?" I asked. I was talking with my mouth full. I needed to know what's going on.

"We were going on a date, and somebody tried to rob KC and messed up his car somehow. It wouldn't start, they had my baby at gunpoint I heard something going on. I had to think quick. I acted like I was going to give the guys whatever they wanted and drop them again. They were of Jamaican descent," Armony confided. It's going to get worse before it gets better. Something is going on.

"Are you fucking serious? Something is going on, damn the very next day. You were at the right place at the right time." I was reassured. I can't believe this shit, better her than me I can't be killing people every fucking day. It's either kill or be killed.

"That's why I wanted to come out here with you, I feel that we can form some type of bond. I don't have many friends and the one that I did have flipped on me. I just feel comfortable around you for some reason. You're annoying, though." Armony confided. I could tell that Killany was a real chick, you can tell a fraud from a mile away.

"I'm annoying, and you are too. I don't have any friends, but my sisters. I'm open to forming a bond with you. I don't have anything against you, but keep Menya away from me, she's not your friend, I don't how you can't see that." I revealed. Armony, might not be that bad, she's pretty cool, but I'll never tell her that. I finished eating my food. I looked at my phone I had a text.

Bae: *You think this is game, huh?? I told you to unblock me, and you haven't done that so I'm locking you out of your phone until I feel like it.*

This man is crazy, what did I get myself into. Who hacks somebody's phone because they're on block.

"What's wrong Killany?" Armony asked. Her whole vibe just changed within seconds.

"Here, look at my phone." I offered. I passed my phone to Armony so she could see what the fuck I was talking about.

"I forgot to tell you to unblock him because they have a hacker that works for them and he can hack anything even Apple, KC did that to me before. I would try to make a call, and all my calls were routed to him. Let me make a call and see. Oh shit, he has you locked out of your phone." Armony I remembered. Yung has lost it. He's crazy.

"I don't have time for this shit. What do you want to do? Mall, massage and go out for drinks and food later?" I declared. Yung was a little too crazy for my liking. I don't know if this relationship would be healthy for me. I conduct business off of my phone clients call me, and he knows that.

Future: *What about my clients that call me, how will they get in touch with me?*

Bae: *Email!*

Chapter 25

Killany

Yung and I were going out on a date tonight. We hadn't seen each other in about two weeks since our last encounter in Atlanta when we hopped on a flight to Virginia. We made love until we both tapped out. I woke up and he was gone, I was pissed because I couldn't believe he did that shit. I missed him something serious. I missed my home though even though I don't have any family here. I loved Virginia, it was so peaceful and quiet. It's a nice place to raise a family. I don't know what I was going to wear tonight. He swore he knew my city and he was taking me somewhere I've never been before. Yung never ceases to amaze me. We complete each other I didn't quite know if I was really ready to be in a relationship or not. Commitment scares the shit out of me. Every other day we are arguing about something.

I'm so used to doing me, and I don't know if I can adapt to that type of change. I asked my mother what should I do, and she said dealing with Yung, he needs a rider. He's a savage in these streets, he needs somebody that can hold him down and be there for him when the going gets tough, and I'm more than capable of doing that. It was time for me to boss up and come into my own and stopped being worried what my father would think. My mother assured me that everything would be fine and don't blow it because he was the one and you only get one shot. I wanted to tell her momma are you serious about blowing it, because you and my dad just got back together after twenty-one years.

Yung and I have been dating for about two months. I feel as if lately we haven't spent enough time with each other. He's been busy, and I have too. I guess he missed me because he showed up on my doorstep with white roses. We just put a title on what we're doing. I'm not really feeling the long-distance shit, but that's cool because we still planned on moving in together soon. Armony stayed out here for a few days, and we actually had fun. Her birthday party was next week, and she invited me to her party, I was definitely showing my face.

He wanted me to move to New Jersey, and I was willing to do that. I wasn't giving up my place in Virginia though. I'm flying to Atlantic City this weekend for Armony's birthday party. Yung wanted me to come. Ray said Cartier invited her so she would be there, her flight leaves at four PM. We got us a suite together. Ugh, I can't stand Menya; Armony's friend, she's a hood rat in disguise. Ray beat that ass; I will never forget it. I don't have any friends, so I don't care to know Menya. I'll be cordial for the sake of Armony, KC, and Yung, but other than that no. She's loud and obnoxious, but let her ratchet side come out. That's Armony's girl ugh, and she used to date Cartier, and she was saying some slick shit on our last encounter. I had to let her know. Ray put them hands on her. I don't care what she and Cartier did on their time, but as long as he doesn't break my sister's heart we good. She was looking crazy, and I was like bitch what you can't hold a candle to mine.

Yung

I pulled up on Killany I missed her the two weeks we spent apart was too fucking long. I've been handling my business, I guess you don't really miss a person until you're not in their presence anymore. I guess that was what was happening to me. I've never been in a real relationship before, she would have to teach me a few things. I planned on taking her on a date tonight at this restaurant on the water my partner BG's uncle owns it. She thinks she knows everything about Virginia, but I can guarantee you she hasn't been here before. She was taking forever to get dressed. She was beautiful, she didn't have to dress up for me. I knew what she looked cleaned up and to be honest, I didn't want another nigga to witness that. I'm so glad her and Armony finally bonded the two of them together was a fucking disaster waiting to happen. I haven't mentioned it to Killany yet, but this week would be her last week in Virginia. I needed her lying next to me every night. She said she was cool with us moving in together we would see.

"I'm ready Yung, how do I look?" Killany asked. I just put on some jeans and a blazer because it gets cold at night. I wanted to be comfortable dealing with Yung, a normal night is never in the cards.

"It took you that long to throw on that? You look good, though, you ready to roll?" I asked. I'm glad she didn't get overdressed I won't have to kill anybody tonight.

"Where are we going?" Killany asked. I love to bug Yung he

gets so mad.

"Be patient, and you'll see," I warned. Damn, she's nosey.

"Excuse me, I was just asking. Do you want me to drive?" Killany offered. Yung can be real rude at times.

"Thanks, but no thanks, I want to drive you around, is that ok? Get in the car, please. Can I do that Killany?" I asked. I pulled off from her house and headed in the direction of the restaurant. It was about thirty minutes from her house. She's pushing it. I think she loves to push me just to hear me snap. I had a nice night planned for us, I wanted to enjoy it. I haven't relaxed in over two weeks. I wanted to eat, give Killany the keys to our new house, and take a walk on the beach that's it.

"You sure can." Killany smiled. Yung is doing too much. Let me chill before this whole night goes left before it evens start. I'll chill out for now because it doesn't take much to get him thrown off in one of his moods. I would've preferred to stay in, cook, lay on his chest, and twerk on that dick, but since he wants to go out I'll accompany him. My dad is dying to meet him, but I wasn't ready for that. My dad is so judgmental he didn't think anybody was good enough for his daughters.

"We finally arrived at No Frill Bar and Grill it was a nice setup. I knew she'd never been here before because I could tell by her facial expression. I wanted to surprise her and cater to her a little bit. I missed her at the house she would cook a nigga breakfast, lunch, and dinner. I knew she would be a great mother to my children. I planned on knocking her up soon, I didn't want any twins either." I thought to myself.

"Yung, I've never been here before. I've wanted to come for months I just never got around to it. The décor is sick; black and gold it's designed like a palace. "Killany mentioned. I heard the food here was amazing. The reviews were great, I couldn't wait to see the menu.

"I know Killany that's why I wanted to bring you here. I want to do things that you've never done before. I want to be your first and last everything from here on out. Can I do that?" I asked. She knows what type of guy I am. I don't do things that everybody does. I'm Yung I do what the fuck I want whenever I want. I make shit happen. I'm not a procrastinator. Our waiter escorted us to a private area I had reserved just for us on the beach. The sun had just set, it glared at our table. Our food was already waiting for us. I ordered a variety of things that I knew Killany would love.

"Yung, you know you can do that," Killany admitted. Yung swore he was the bosses of all bosses and nobody moved like him. I loved his confidence. He's really outdone himself this time. I can't believe he had all of this setup for us. I've been here twice already, but I wouldn't tell him that. I'll let him feel like he's doing something. He does have a lot of qualities that I do admire. He reminded me of my father a lot. I knew my dad would like him, but then again, he might not because my mother used to date his uncle. I would never put that out there.

"Close your mouth Killany I know you're surprised. I want you to sit directly in front of me. I have a couple of gifts that I want to give you before we decide to eat our food." I joked. She wasn't expecting that shit.

"Whatever Yung, I've been a really good girl, huh? I'm getting

130

gifts what's the occasion? You don't have any bitches stashed anywhere." Killany smirked. What the fuck is he up too? We've been doing good without any fuck ups.

"Killany, you know me better than that. I'm the realest nigga you'll ever meet, trust me. I have two gifts for you. I tossed her the keys to our new home. I gave her a second set of keys which was the keys to her cocaine white Mercedes G-Wagon." I boasted. I'm that nigga, she'll never forget me as long as she lives.

"Yung, what are these keys for? Killany asked. What's really going on? One set of keys that I was given has a Mercedes key fob attached. So, I knew off top, that was a car, but the other set of keys looked like a fresh pair of door keys or some keys to a safe or vault. I couldn't be too sure dealing with Yung.

"The first set of keys are the keys to our new home and the second set of keys belongs to your new Cocaine White Mercedes G Wagon, you've been eyeing it for a minute, so I had to get that for you. You've been a good girl you deserve it." I revealed. I didn't want to do any half stepping with Killany, some may think it's too soon, but when it's real you can't put a time limit on anything you move how you see fit and that how I move. If you could see her facial expression that confirms that I've done everything right.

"I've been a good girl huh? You've been a really good man too. I appreciate everything that you do for me. You sure you're ready to wake up next to me every morning and smell my breath. That also includes me lying on your chest a night." Killany smiled. I continued to eat my food. Yung is definitely the man. I'm grateful that we found each other. I won't take him for granted.

"I been doing it, ain't shit changed, but I have some mints on the side of your bed." I laughed. Killany knows her breath be humming in the morning. We ate our food, and everything was good. We made our way to the beach; the waves were deep, and the sun had just set. I had my arms wrapped around her. I was ready to get back to her place. I need to get my dick wet, it's been two long weeks, and I needed to release some stress. I was backed up and standing behind Killany with her ass pressed against my dick wasn't going to work. I needed her face down, ass up.

"Tonight, was actually kind of romantic. I was ready to go home, so me and Yung can get to it. I missed him something serious, and I couldn't wait to show him. I felt his dick smack me on my ass a few times he needs to learn how to control that big monster. I would enjoy this time while it lasted because we haven't had a free night in very long time." Killany I thought to myself.

"Virginia is pretty cool, but it's not Jersey. I don't want you to get home sick again and run off on a nigga. Can you promise me that?" I begged. That last little stunt that Killany pulled threw me off.

"I'm good as long you don't give me a reason to leave, you know how you do. I figured that I could venture out in Jersey and find some potential clients also and expand my business. I have it figured out already, some of the small businesses in Jersey Gardens and the retail space in the vicinity. I would extend them a proposal also included with my prices and what my services included." Killany suggested. Moving to Jersey was cool, but I needed some clients out there. I love to work, and I needed to expand my horizon that was my plan. Yung's always working, so I was going to work too. I don't care how much money he had. I still needed my own.

"Oh ok, I see you. You making plans and moves huh? What if I didn't want you to work? I wanted you to stay at home and focus on me. Could you do that for me?" I asked. One thing that I love about Killany is she's a hustler at heart. She already has her plans in motion, she's not sitting back waiting for me to do nothing.

"Hell no, I can't do that I have skills and talent that I would never waste. I'm passionate about what I do. You shouldn't even have asked me to do that. I need to tap in the Jersey market and see what they have to offer. I will work from home, though," Killany said. Yung knew I could never sit back and just focus on him. I wouldn't be complete if I had to choose between him and work.

"I was just fucking with you. I love your ambition, I'm ready to get up out of here you ready to go? Now you can drive. I need to get you up out of these clothes asap." I laughed. Killany just went in.

Chapter 26

Raven

Cartier invited me to KC's party in Atlantic City for the weekend. I was in the process of packing my bags, but he insisted on buying me whatever when I got there. That was cool and all but between my dad and Tariq I had way too much money and clothes. Kaniya thought that I was her personal Barbie doll, she would bring clothes that she wanted to wear, but couldn't because she was pregnant, anything that Cartier would do for me is extra. Tariq wasn't too fond of me dating, but oh well. I was cool with flying out there for the weekend because I would get to see Killany. The last time I saw her was a few weeks ago, when Yung came to Onyx in Atlanta and showed his ass. I couldn't deal with her, and Kaniya those two do the most and will get somebody killed. I don't know who's the worst. Cartier and I hung out that same night, we still hadn't had sex yet. I assumed that he was getting it from somewhere else. I wasn't ready yet, and I don't know if I could actually do the long-distance thing yet.

Killany told me to live a little. Another thing that scares me too is that Killany has already endured a bunch of shit that I don't know if I'm ready for. I've never killed anybody, I know how to use a gun, I never wanted to be anybody's ride or die chick, I'm not riding for no nigga and dying for no nigga period. I liked Cartier a lot, but I didn't want to be forced to deal with the street shit. This would be my first time in Jersey, I hope I don't run into any of Cartier's ex's, side chicks, or whatever. I couldn't wait to see what the city had to offer. It was an all-black affair. My flight leaves at one PM, and Killany would pick me up from there.

Cartier

I invited Raven out to my city for the weekend to Kc's party. I liked her a whole lot. I was trying to take my time with her and be patient and shit. She was young, I wouldn't say naïve, but I could tell that she didn't know that much about the streets. She was a good girl, but if she wanted to be with a boss like me, she would have to come up out of her shell. I wanted to be her first and last everything. I was living foul, but I wasn't committed to anybody except for Ben Franklin, that's one bitch that will never disappoint me. I had a few chicks that I bust down on a weekly to get my fix, but I'll disappoint those hoes quick if Raven was mine, but it'll happen. I wanted her in the worst way too. I was pissed that she and Killany had a room together. I wanted her to come to my house and stay the weekend. I definitely need to holla at Yung about that shit. I like Killany and all but don't make reservations for my girl and shit. Let me do that I wanted to reserve Raven in my bed and shit.

"What, CJ the fuck you want?" Yung laughed.

"Fuck you, weak ass nigga call Killany and tell her too dead that room her and Raven got booked I need Ray with me tonight and not with her." I laughed. I need Killany to get on board.

"Oh ok, I didn't know shit about Killany having a room booked, she got me fucked up I'll handle her hard head ass in a minute, you must be trying to get some pussy tonight?" Yung laughed. Cartier thought he was slick, he should've told Ray that he wanted her to stay with him, end of discussion.

"No, I'm not on that with her, Yung, if she wants to give it to me then I won't turn it down. I'll give her something that she'll never forget, death stroke, she'll fuck around and have my kids." I laughed. I'm serious I could settle down with Raven it's just something about her I don't know what it is yet.

Yung

I promise you Killany is one hard headed motherfucker, she hasn't told me anything about her booking a room and staying there. When did she start that shit, she likes playing with me and shit I'm one nigga that she should think twice about playing with. I promise you I don't think she's built for this shit, she can never follow my lead on nothing she always wants to do her own shit, and that doesn't sit well with me. I'm a fucking boss, and I live a savage ass life the last thing that I need is for her to do anything that I tell her not to do. Let me call and check her ass about this bullshit she's trying to pull.

"Yeah, Yung what's up?" Killany cackled. I'm trying to get my stuff together I don't have time to be on the phone, he already played me a few weeks ago, when he up and left.

"Get that bass up out of your voice. When I call, you don't use that tone you should say yes baby, I heard you booked you and Ray a room for what? The fuck you trying to do,"I yelled. I know she was in her feelings about that shit that happened a few weeks ago, but we were pass that shit, yeah, I made love to her and left as soon as I put her to sleep. I'm a savage ass nigga, that's what the fuck I do.

"I did book us a room, she wanted to see the city? Is that a problem with you baby?" Killany sassed. I had to look at my phone I couldn't believe Yung was tripping like this too hard. He didn't confirm that he wanted me to stay with them either.

"I do have a problem with it. Since when do you come to Jersey and stay in a hotel? I feel that you are being spiteful, let me ask you this Killany, who has the dick in the relationship me or you and it's for damn sure not you. Listen to what the fuck I tell you to do, and we can go a lot further, your room is canceled. Call Ray and tell her she's staying with Cartier for the weekend and I'll see you in a few hours," I said. This girl drives me insane, she's hard headed, she knew that shit wouldn't be cool with me.

Killany

I don't know who Yung thought he was, but I'm tired of him talking to me like I'm his child last I checked he didn't have any. It's always his way or no way. Yes, he invited me to the party and no I never stay at a hotel, but my sister is coming so I wanted to spend some time with her what's wrong with that. Let me call Ray and let her know it's a change of plans COURTESY of Yung and Cartier.

"What's up Killany you miss already?" Raven laughed into the phone.

"Girl, don't flatter yourself. It's a change of plans Yung canceled our room you're staying with Cartier. Did you tell Cartier we had a room? Yung never knew, I guess your man felt some type of way about it and had Yung to call me with the shit so whatever I didn't even feel like arguing with him and shit. Are you cool with staying the weekend with Cartier?" I blurted out. I had to run this shit by Ray to see if she was cool with what just transpired.

"Oh ok, so you're saying that Cartier got this started because I wasn't staying with him? I don't see why he's mad because he didn't offer me to stay with him. I thought he had some shit to hide, but we'll see I'm about to call him, though. I love you sis, and I'll see you in a few," Raven said. Cartier so full of it I don't understand why he didn't just ask me. Now he's thrown Killany and Yung in the mix knowing damn well those two are crazy and too much alike.

Raven

I understand where Cartier is coming from because he invited me to the party. He never offered me to come and stay with him either, but I'm about to call his sneaky ass. I thought we communicated enough that we didn't need anybody in our business. Let me call him, though.

"Hey, Ray baby, what's up with you?" Cartier smiled. I rubbed my hands together like Birdman. I guess my plan worked with Yung.

"I just got a call from Killany she was upset Yung canceled our room. If you wanted me to stay with you for the weekend, you should've said something. I thought you had some shit to hide that's why you didn't offer. I thought our communication level was strong enough where we didn't need anybody involved in what we have going on. I guess I thought wrong, though," I stated. Cartier thought he was slick. I brought some bad ass lingerie Kaniya helped me pick out just in case, he might get all of me tonight he might not, but just in case I was ready.

"Ray, let me keep it ninety-five with you. I should've asked you, BUT I didn't think that I had too. Anytime we are in each other's presence shit, I want to be with you. I shouldn't have called Yung and had him to get at Killany. I'm sorry for that, but it is what is. I don't have shit to hide, you and I aren't committed to each other that's your choice and not mine. Do I have chicks that I smash from time to time? Yes, I do, and I strap up twice, and they all know about you. Do they know where I lay my head at, no because they ain't you," Cartier retorted. I didn't care about Raven spitting that hot ass shit she already knew what it was. What's understood doesn't need to be explained.

"I hear you Cartier; a closed mouth doesn't get fed. I'll see you in a few." I interrupted. I can't believe he just tried to flip this shit on me. I guess he was feeling himself, he wanted me to know about all of the chicks he was bussing down.

"I love you Raven. I want to be with you, stop playing with a nigga." Cartier revealed. I put myself out there. I think I wanted Ray because she wasn't your average chick. She was young but not dumb. I couldn't trick her out of her pussy. I had to earn it, every inch of her. She had me working overtime too.

"I love you too Cartier, I'll see you later ok." Raven smiled.

Cartier

I could tell Raven was in her feelings about what I just said, but oh well. I'm a real ass nigga I don't have to lie about shit I do. I kept if ninety- five with her. I'll expect her to do the same with me. She isn't as innocent as people think she is. Raven is sneaky just like her sisters. I follow her on Instagram and Facebook, she converses with a few cats too. I have eyes on her that she doesn't know about it. I want to be with Ray, but I won't beg her or force her.

I want her to want me to be her man. I won't wait forever, though. I know she's in her feelings, but I can't change that. I planned on locking her down this weekend, no if and buts about it. I had my hoes in line. I prayed they didn't act stupid because Ray would beat their ass. My mom wanted to meet her. I would arrange something in the future. I need to get Killany an I'm sorry gift since Yung dug deep in her ass, she'll forgive me later, she knew what time it was anyway. She'll be alright she was running game anyway, she knew Yung wouldn't let that shit fly. It's funny to see Yung committed, he was acting a fool over Killany, she was a good look for him. Shorty wild though I couldn't wait to see Ray later.

Chapter 27

Killany

My flight was delayed so I would actually be meeting Ray at the airport. The pilot just announced we were about to land. If I weren't trying to change my ways, me and Ray would dip and still get our suite, but Yung is too crazy, and I just don't feel like dealing with the drama. We have a love and hate relationship, I love him today and hate him tomorrow. I couldn't wait to see Armony, I brought her a gift I'm sure she would like it. We just landed, I don't know how this conversation is going to go with Yung after the conversation we just had. I grabbed my luggage and made my way to exit the plane. Ray was flying Southwest also, so I was going to wait on her, her flight just landed also.

I took my phone off airplane mode. I had six missed text, and I had several text messages from Yung asking where I was? Have I made it yet and where I was located? I wasn't even feeling Yung right now because our little conversation a few hours ago, I'm still tripping off that. Yung and I were official, I thought he would be cool with Ray and I staying together just for the weekend. I agreed to move in with him so I wasn't returning back to Virginia, I was staying here.

"Hey who pissed in your cheerios I'm here," Raven said. Lord, Killany still in her feelings about that lil' bullshit Cartier did earlier. He needs to apologize.

"Hey Ray, I'm sorry I was just thinking about something, I'm good and you? You look so pretty." I complemented her. I didn't even notice when Raven arrived. I'm not even paying attention and shit.

"I'm sorry about earlier. I didn't mean to cause problems between you and Yung I know how crazy he gets." Raven reassured. I hate Cartier did that, and he knows his brother is crazy and acts up for no reason.

"You're good I'm over it, and I hope Yung is too. He already sent me a text and said they were outside waiting on us already," I mentioned. Cartier and Raven needed some alone time anyway. I missed my body pillow, Yung. The party **starts at ten** PM, I have plenty of time to nap and get dressed.

"Damn, they're outside already?" Raven complained. I at least wanted to have lunch with my sister maybe even go to the mall. I can't even catch my breath good.

"Yes, they are already outside waiting for us." I smiled. Raven has no idea. We made our way in the direction toward where Yung and Cartier were waiting for us. We hopped on a train to take us to the location where they would be waiting. I didn't pack anything because I wasn't planning on going back home. I had plenty of clothes that I left here anyway. Armony shot me a text also to see if I made it yet. I'll hit her back as soon as I get with Yung and situated.

"Where's your luggage?" Raven inquired. Killany didn't bring shit, but a MCM backpack and I'm sure her laptop is in there and her gun.

"I didn't bring any I'm staying out here for a while, and I have plenty of clothes at Yung's already, no need to bring extra shit," I informed her. Raven is so damn nosy she doesn't miss shit. I spotted

Yung and Cartier, damn Yung looks fuck able right now. I tapped Ray and pointed in their direction so she could see Cartier.

"Cartier, is really handsome, straight like that huh? I really like Yung for you. I wanted to have lunch and hangout before you get booed up. Looks like that won't be happening now. What are you wearing to the party?" Raven asked. I haven't been alone with Cartier in a while, maybe two months. I hope I don't run into any bullshit.

"I don't know yet. Something simple though because you just never know what can happen. I'm wearing some booties, though. I stay prepared, shit has been crazy lately more than you'll ever know. "I cautioned. I'm dressing down, still cute, but relaxed just in case I have to put in some work. I'm not even taking a drink. We finally made it to the exit. Yung and I went our way, and so did Cartier and Ray.

"Bye Killany Denise," Raven mimicked. She hated when we called her that. I was waiting for her to flip me a bird, and she did it. I fell out laughing.

Raven

I haven't been in Jersey for an hour, and he's already tripping. Cartier's phones have been blowing up and mine too. As soon as I decided to shoot somebody a text back, he wants to have an attitude, for what though we're not together, since our little run-in at the club he's been acting real crazy. He thought he was slick, Tariq already told he had somebody watching me because he keeps security on me also. I don't know what that was about. I've been dating a couple of guys, I'm only twenty-one, so I was going to act as such and have fun. Cartier was twenty-four, and he assured me he was doing him. I couldn't understand why he was mad at me doing me.

Yes, I wanted that hood love, but not right now, Killany and Kaniya go through too much dealing with their men of choice, so that's why I was making my choice to continue to be single. If Cartier had an issue with that, then we could stop dating altogether. I'm not ready to endure everything that my sisters go through if I don't have too. This nigga had the nerve to grab my fucking phone out of my hand, fuck no.

"Who in the fuck is JC?" Cartier contended. Raven is about to make me lay hands on her with this extra friendly shit. I can't even look at her after reading this text.

"A friend," I sassed. Why is he tripping, knowing damn well he has friends that he keeps company with? He's crazy too, I can't deal with this extra shit.

"A friend huh? He said he love you? Why is he begging to be with you and see you again? Let me call this nigga and ask him? It's more than what the fuck you telling me just off these texts alone." Cartier argued. Raven's sneaky as fuck.

"Hey baby, I love you. When will I see yo' fine ass again? I want to be with you," JC answered. Raven got me gone, and she doesn't even know it.

"You love her? You want to be with her? You won't see her anymore, trust me. Did she tell you she had a man?" Cartier exclaimed. I can't believe this shit, this nigga is really professing his love to Raven. She better hope that nigga say the right shit, if not I'm going to choke her ass up for playing with a nigga like me.

"Hell yeah, I love her, and I want to be with her. Last I checked she was a free agent. Unless she tells me otherwise I'm not easing up I'll forever try my luck. I don't give a fuck about what you screaming," JC argued. I had to look at this phone and hang it up. I know he didn't call me questioning me about a woman that's not his or mine. I knew she was going to Jersey to kick it with him so what that shit didn't matter to me.

"I told you it was nothing." I sassed. I don't even know why he's tripping. He's doing entirely too much. I don't care if he's mad so fucking what. He just openly admitted he was fucking different broads. You mad because another guy is interested in me.

"You ain't told me shit. I want to be with you Ray, but I ain't gon' sweat you. Why does he think he has a chance? You want to know why because you're giving that nigga hope. Why you doing that shit? If I'm not worth it and you ain't trying to establish shit you can take your ass back home." Cartier said. I'm not being nobody's side nigga. If Raven wanted to play games, she could play that shit by her damn self.

Chapter 28

Cartier

I don't even know why I'm tripping so hard especially behind some pussy I haven't even touched or tasted. Ray is young, though, and she has some growing to do, but I was cool on her, and she can do her. I know what to expect from her. She can take her sneaky ass back to Georgia and that fuck nigga. I hate I even canceled her room because she can stay there tonight. I'll tell Yung to pick her up from my house because she ain't riding with me. I don't even want her coming back to my house. It's too many females out here that want me, and I'm caught up on her, that shit is a wrap today. I'll show her. She's giving niggas hope I can give a lot of bitches hopes and dreams too. I had more than just Menya lined up too. I was speeding to get to Yung, so I can drop her off. Let me call Yung and see where they are so she can kick it with her sister.

"What CJ, what you want?" Yung answered. Damn, he calling me already.

"Have you and Killany made it to the crib? I need to drop Ray off over there with her unfaithful and sneaky behind." I explained. I can't get over this shit mainly because she was doing me how I do other females.

"Cartier, don't fucking go there. What you won't do is talk about me like I'm not sitting next to you. You don't have to take me anywhere, take to me to the room I reserved. I don't have to be anywhere that I'm not wanted." Raven argued. I can't believe he really is this mad. When did we make it official? I missed that part.

"CJ, man, chill out I'm headed to the crib now," Yung mentioned. What happened between those two? What did Raven do? I have never known for CJ to get mad or upset behind any female besides my OG and our little sister.

Raven

I can't believe him. It's cool for him to dish shit out but he can't take in return. I'm tired of him putting Yung in our business every time. We're not together I don't see what's the problem. He wants to be with me, but I'm not ready for that just yet. He had the nerve to call JC and question him about what the fuck we had going on. JC held his own don't let that college boy look fool you. I like JC, and he's local too. Why does it matter, you live in Jersey and I live in Georgia? I'm not grabbing his phones to see who's calling him, what would I do that for. I could tell that he wanted to lay hands on me, I swear I would've killed him in this car. He had the nerve to say I'm not gon' sweat you. Who asked you to, because I didn't? I can't wait to get to this party because I know he on some spiteful shit, but I will be too. He better recognize what blood flows through me. After I shut this party down, I'm catching a flight back home. It's a wrap for Cartier and me I'm not doing this shit with him. He can do him, and I'll do me. I'm anxious I don't even want to get Killany involved, her and Yung already go through too much. I wasn't telling her my plans. I wish he would stop looking at me and drive. I applied some more lip gloss to my pouty lips and pulled out my other phone and started snapping up. He was heated, yeah bitch I got two phones like Kevin Gates.

"Oh, you got two phones? You think this shit is game huh? Raven I will fucking hurt you stop playing with me." Cartier's voice boomed. She got me fucked up. I pulled this Camaro over right on the side of the road, got out and walked over to the passenger side and opened her door. I motioned with my hand for Raven to get the fuck out.

"We are really about to do this on the side of the road. I turned my location on my iPhone on so Killany could see. I shot her a text to come quick. I don't know what was about to happen and I probably will get locked up fucking with him. I made my way out of the car." I thought to myself.

"I pulled her towards me and got all up in her face. You like playing with a nigga like me huh? I'm crazy Ray, I'm not playing with a full deck. You don't believe that I will hurt you. I don't play about two fucking things; my paper and my heart and I feel like you grabbing that motherfucker and thumping it, but before I let you do that I'll fuck you up and kill that fuck nigga JC that want you. Do you fucking understand me? I was choking her ass." Cartier warned. I told her from the jump don't lie to me or play with me keep it real about that shit you got going on don't have me out here fucking blind.

"Get the fuck up off of me, you are choking me. I've never lied to you about shit that I do, but it's cool for you to tell me about all the bitches you fuck. It ain't no fun when the rabbit got the gun huh? I'mma tell you this you now, you better kill me or do what the fuck you need to do because if you let me go, I will cut your fucking eyes out." I threatened. It's a wrap I'm doing this shit anymore. I'm taking my ass home. I noticed Yung and Killany pulling up. Killany jumped out the car while it was still running.

"CJ, get the fuck up off of her, man. I raised you better than that shit. Fuck around and get your ass locked up out here with these crackers." Yung warned. I can't believe my little brother out here laying hands on a female. If Raven can take him there, they definitely don't need to be together. It's not worth it.

"Ray, are you ok? What the fuck happened let's go. Why in the fuck are you laying hands on my sister Cartier? We are going back to the house, Yung?" Killany screamed. I smacked him in the back of his head. Oh, hell no I'm going to shoot his ass. I don't play about men hitting or choking females.

"I'm good he didn't hit me, he just choked me." I blurted. I had to clear that shit up he didn't hit me at all. Cartier was in his feelings that don't overshadow his actions, but that's what it was.

"She ain't going no fucking where, but with me, let's go Ray. I don't know why in the fuck she called you two anyway. I was just letting her know don't play with my heart. That shit ain't cool. Being friendly with a nigga will get him killed, and her feelings hurt. Killany you know that shit first hand so you can excuse yourself. What we have going on has nothing to do with you." Cartier interrupted. I like Killany, but mind your fucking business and let me tend to mine.

"Ray, are you good? Let me know, and you can roll with us. I don't give a fuck what CJ spitting. If you're not with it, then get in the car, and we can roll." Yung asked. I wanted to laugh so bad, CJ just read Killany's ass talking about that friendly shit she was doing last month. I can't wait to check his ass about that shit.

"I'm good Yung we just had a misunderstanding. I didn't mean to get you two involved. I love you Killany doesn't worry about me I'll be alright. We'll see you guys later." I said. Cartier just went nuts. Cartier and I got back in the car and headed in the direction of his house I assumed.

***

We finally made to Cartier's house. All I wanted to do was take a hot shower and lay down for a few. I can't believe I just went through this shit. I hope and pray Killany's big mouth self don't tell Kaniya, Tariq, or my dad because they will be on their way. It was the afternoon of the party, Cartier and I still had a lot of tension between us. Thank God, Yung and Killany pulled up it was a mess. He was choking me and shit. It's like he snapped. I tried to leave with Killany and Yung, but he refused. I was at his house getting ready. I just got out the shower. I pulled the shower curtain back, and Cartier was sitting on the toilet smoking. I needed to hit that shit he was smoking on it smelt good. I was scared because I've never been naked in front of a guy before. The last time Cartier respected my privacy, but this time he was invading my privacy. The bathroom was dark and gloomy because of the rain, I was using natural light.

"Come Here Ray, I'm sorry I didn't mean to do that shit to you earlier. It's just that I love you and to know that you giving niggas hope that it can be you and them instead of you and me, fucks with my mental. I want you to be the air that I breathe." Cartier confided. I had to confess and keep that shit real, I would never mislead her in any type of way.

"I love you too Cartier, please believe me when I say that I do, I didn't give him hope that it could be us because it'll always be Ray and Cartier before anything," I revealed. I love Cartier I do, but I'm not quite ready to be in a relationship, that would be new to me. That's something I've never been in. We're already arguing and fighting. I attempted to wrap a towel around me.

"Don't cover up, come here, Ray," Cartier begged. I wanted her in the worst way, tonight was definitely the night she was going to be mine, and I wasn't having it no other way.

"Why not? I'm not comfortable with you looking at me while I'm naked." I murmured. Cartier was looking at me like a piece of meat. I wasn't ready, but if it happened it did. I was prepared shit I dreamed about this.

"Is it mine? I grabbed her clit." Cartier asked. I started playing in her pussy damn she was tight, her walls put a lock on my finger. I brought my fingers toward my nose her pussy smelt just like water. I wanted her to taste herself.

"Yes, it's yours." I babbled. Cartier was playing with my pussy it was feeling so good. I didn't want him to stop. My knees started to shake.

Kaniya told me when she was prepping me on what to do just in case it happened. Don't just lay there move your body a little and then you'll find your rhythm. I found it, and I was grinding up against him like it was going to be my last time.

"It's mine Ray? If we take it there, it's no coming back from this. No friends, it's just you and me forever." Cartier claimed. She nodded her head yes. I wanted to be gentle with Ray she welcomed her body to me finally. I lifted her body up. I held her pussy over my mouth, she held on to the shower rod for support. I was dying to taste her. It was so wet and pure just like the Niagara Falls. I was a bull attacking my prey. I applied pressure on her clit with my tongue and gave her some face action, her juices came raining down on my face, she just came. I made my way to my bedroom, my arms were secured on her hips. I made sure I was extra careful. I wanted to continue to eat her while on the way to the bedroom. I could tell she was little shaken up. I laid her on the bed, and I positioned myself between her legs they were spread wide open. I've been wanting to do this for the longest. I hope I opened her up because she was extra tight. I slowly began to make way inside. I had to take it easy on her, she started to squirm a little.

I had the tip in, damn her pussy was tight. It was now or never, I made my way in she was saying it hurts. I kissed the pain away. She kissed me back, she was getting relaxed. I wanted her first time to be special and passionate she was a little more comfortable now. I went in for the kill she was throwing that pussy back at a nigga. My sheets were soaked. My room was filled with soft moans, and both of our bodies were getting acquainted with each other. The faces she was making, didn't do her any justice. I had to slow it down because I didn't want to nut too fast, I tried to ease up out the pussy, but her walls just kept sucking me in.

"My very first time, I can't believe Cartier, and I just went there. I wouldn't have it any other way. I wish we hadn't argued or fought prior. He knew what he was doing, I wanted it, though. It's official Cartier, and I are a couple. I hope I don't regret this shit later. The way he ate my pussy from the front and back It felt so good. I've heard horror stories of women bleeding on their first encounter, thank God that didn't happen to me. I was sore, though, Cartier was so big I wanted to scream. We kept at it for about an hour." I thought to myself. I have to keep it real with JC we can't kick it or none of that shit. Cartier has to let his ducks know what it is too. I need all of him not part of him. He was pissed that somebody else was occupying my time other than him. I really liked JC it's good that it ended before it started. I was feeling Cartier from the moment we first met each other.

Chapter 29

Armony

It was the eve of my birthday. It's my birthday I can bitch and be petty if I want too, yeah that part. I was so ecstatic, my birthday is a fucking holiday, seriously. KC really went all out with this one. He rented out the Crowne Plaza; my party will be held there. My colors were Maroon and Black. I've received so many phone calls and texts, I really felt loved. My mother and father spoiled me also. Yeah, I'm a brat so what. I was looking forward to my party tonight. The crew will be in attendance. I haven't actually spoken to Raven, but I did want to reach out and apologize to her for my actions in New Orleans. I haven't heard from Menya, I'm sure she will show her face because my party was the talk of the city. Trust me when I tell you I was coming through like Beyoncé and KC was Jay-Z.

I invited Killany to have a spa date with me she declined. She said her and Yung were making up for lost times. We have actually gotten a lot closer, that's my bitch no matter what. I'm glad we linked up, these past few months we have gone through so much together. I wouldn't change it for nothing. She's definitely VIP. It was a little after seven PM, and it was time for me to get suited and snatched, beat to the gods. I'm not exactly sure what my attire would be for tonight. I had three options. My glam squad would be arriving any minute. Twenty-eight looks good on me. I was coming of age, one thing about time you get better with it. When it's your time, it's your time, and nobody can take that from you. I was living my life to the fullest, working on having a baby making sure my boutique flourishes. I actually felt good about tonight you can never be too sure. I'm always prepared if shit goes left. My glam squad just arrived. It's time to get dolled up.

Kaniya

Killany called me and told me what the fuck happened to Raven. Yung was in the background talking shit. He didn't like me for some reason. I don't care, I wasn't losing any sleep. It was very comical to me because Yung couldn't have known who he was lying next to at night because Killany talks too fucking much. She doesn't care about telling anybody's business, that's a hobby of hers, but she'll make sure her own is secret safe. That's probably why she didn't have any fucking friends now that I think about it. I've been calling Raven's phone for over three hours now, and she hasn't answered. I sent her a text to let her know I was on my way. I wasn't about to tell Tariq because he was on papers and liable to kill Cartier and he would be sent back to jail. He swears Raven is his daughter. I definitely wasn't about to tell my dad. I don't play that shit about my little sister period. I make house calls pregnant and all, I was coming to see about mine. I heard it was a party tonight I'll make sure I slay for the occasion. My flight leaves at nine PM. I had my sidepiece Dro coming with me. If creeping with him is wrong, I don't want to be right.

"You're going somewhere?" Tariq questioned.

"Yeah on an expedition," I sassed. I can't believe he was questioning me, move around. I caught his ass on some single shit, I did a pop-up, and some chick was skinning and grinning in his face. He had his hands on her ass. I busted her in her fucking face and him too. Don't play with me. We don't have to do shit you don't want to.

Raven

I took a nap after Cartier, and I had sex, I was tired too. Armony's birthday party was scheduled to start in a few. I needed to get dressed also. Her colors were Maroon and Black, my dress was perfect, and my shoes were astonishing. I heard the shower going. I assumed Cartier already started to get dressed. I'll join him. I checked my phone to see what time it was. I had twelve missed calls from Kaniya and a text stating that she was on her. Killany's wrong for running back and telling her shit knowing damn well it wasn't that serious. She knows Kaniya will cut a fool, now she's on her way for nothing. Let me call Killany and give her piece of my mind.

"Hey, Ray are you getting ready?" Killany smiled. I hoped her, and Cartier got past whatever issues they had earlier.

"Nope not yet. Let me ask you this why did you call Kaniya and tell her what happened between me and Cartier? That shit was foul as fuck!" I shouted. I shouldn't have even sent her a text telling her to come to my rescue thinking that she has changed, but she hasn't.

"I'm sorry Raven, I really am. I tell Kaniya everything, and I just got caught up in the moment. She didn't tell me that she was coming. "Killany admitted. Damn, I messed up, I shouldn't have done that. I wouldn't mind seeing Kaniya's pregnant self anyway.

"I forgive you, I've learned a valuable lesson. I'll see you later, I'm about to get dressed," I sassed. Killany didn't get the picture Kaniya was pregnant and didn't need to be traveling. She's pregnant with twins, for God sake she's high risk.

"Ray, what's wrong, who were you talking to?" Cartier demanded. She was arguing with somebody about something, and I could tell that it has her down by her voice.

"Killany, she told Kaniya about our little run in and now she's on her way she called twelve times while I was sleep," I confessed. When Kaniya comes, she comes hard. When she gets here, I'll explain everything so hopefully, she won't cut up too bad.

"Oh ok, I'm sorry. I'll talk to her when she comes. I really am sorry it'll never happen again. "Cartier confessed. I'll be sure to holla at Kaniya, she's wild Yung told me she pulled that strap out on him. She needs to sit her pregnant self down she won't lil' Bow Wow me.

Killany

Raven, called me she was upset that I called Kaniya and told her what happen. Raven knows that I can't hold water, Kaniya is my confidant. I tell her everything and vice versa. I really am sorry I didn't think that she would actually come here. Her sneaky ass just wanted to creep off for a few days with Dro. She already told me a couple of days ago, that she had spoken with Dro and he was coming this way to his aunt's birthday party and wanted her to come. This was the icing on the cake when I told her what happen. When Tariq catches her, all hell is going to break loose. I told her when she told me they were back having lunch together don't do that because he really likes you and you like him. I couldn't do nothing but shake my head.

"What's wrong Killany? You need to finish getting dressed so we can get out of here," Yung said.

"That was Ray, she's mad that I told Kaniya about what happened earlier and Kaniya's on her way. "I explained. I don't even feel like hearing his mouth, that's too much like right, I'm definitely about to hear it.

"I can't even be mad at her because I told you about running your mouth. It's not that serious for Kaniya to be coming here. Cartier didn't even do much but choke her up a little," Yung argued. Killany talk's too damn much. That's all her and Kaniya do is gossip all day talking about people pretending that it's about their business. I heard her telling Killany the other day about some guy when I saw Tariq or

Lucky again I was going to air out the sneaky little shit she was doing. She was playing niggas like she was a nigga.

KC

It's was Armony's birthday I went all out for her, I would never put a price on what she can and can't have. Armony is my true rider; these past couple of months we've been through a lot, and she's held me down and never complained about it one time. That's why I planned on proposing to her tonight. This party was the talk of the city it was being compared to the Marty Smalls Ball it's one of the biggest parties in the tristate area. I had security beefed up I'm sure people were coming from everywhere to celebrate my baby's birthday. I hired some photographers to take pictures of us. Our house was a mess, they turned it into a studio. I hated people in my house that I didn't know. I wanted to capture the before and after pictures of the party because this was a special day for us. Armony had her glam squad getting her together for her party. My barber was here about to line me up before I put my clothes on. I had to match her fly. I had a black fitted Gucci tuxedo with a maroon button up and Gucci loafers. I couldn't wait to propose to see her reaction. My barber just finished getting me right he was leaving. I made my way towards Armony's walk in closet where her squad was getting her ready. I stood in the door and admired her from afar.

"Hey baby, do you like what you see?" Armony asked. Damn KC looks really good. I need to get these bitches out of our home. I can see the lust on their faces.

"I love what I see. I don't see nobody but you, my vision is you, ma," I boasted. Armony knows I don't want nobody but her she'll find out tonight, though.

"Good, I'll be finished in a few. You look really handsome KC the Baptist. I have to make sure our pictures are perfect," Armony smiled. I can't wait to jump on that dick later and do a split.

Menya

It was Armony's birthday party tonight. I haven't spoken to her since our altercation in New Orleans, she tried to reach out to me, but I was like fuck her. Ray, or whatever her name was, fractured a bone in my face. I was perfectly fine with that. I decided that tonight, on her birthday, I would come for her in the worst way. All eyes would be on me tonight. I remember the dress that she had designed for her birthday, I got the exact same one. I've linked up with a new crew which consisted of Yung and KC's ex's; Nadia and Toya. The games were definitely about to begin. I went and dug these bitches up to help with my bullshit. We were dressed to fucking impress. Call us the messy click because the shit was about to get messy. We walked up in the Crowne Plaza like we owned this motherfucker, bitch what, KC hired photographers, he had a red carpet and everything, he really out did himself. It's too bad that I came to fuck shit up.

"What's the plan? "Toya asked. Menya is nuts I just wanted to come to the party. I wouldn't dare approach Yung and be on some us type of shit, he would kill me where I stood. I took his money too, I'm sure he didn't forget that.

"Let's make our way to VIP, I want Armony and KC to see us. "Nadia revealed. It's been three years since he walked out of my life, I can't get over it. I need closure.

"Girl, I can't walk up in VIP with you two, it'll ruin everything. I'll go first, and once I distract Armony you guys can make your way in and we'll shut shit down." I revealed. These bitches were sillier than I thought.

Armony

We finally made it. My party was litty. We pulled up to the Crowne; photographers were everywhere outside taking pictures. I had a red carpet in front of the entrance. I was anxious to get out. My Gucci custom fitted maroon and black sequin dress fit me like a glove. I paired my attire with Gucci Molina Crystal T-bar heart pumps. I had a natural beat face today, but my lips popped with Maroon mac lipstick. I didn't want to overdo it with the accessories. KC and I walked through like Beyoncé and Jay-Z all eyes were on us. This party was filled to capacity. I greeted my guest and thanked everybody for coming out and showing me some love. We made our way to my VIP area it was surrounded by nothing but family and close associates, my dad and mom came through for a few, Killany, Yung, Cartier and Ray were in attendance, we were all vibing, the DJ was playing Rihanna *Needed Me.*

> *Didn't they tell you that I was a savage*
> *Didn't they tell you that I was a savage*
> *Fuck you in a white horse in carriage*

"I'd like to say a few words; I need everybody's attention. Armony, come here. I brought you guys out tonight to celebrate Armony's birthday. I wanted to say a little extra, if that's cool with you. Armony you've been thugging it out with me for three years. It hasn't been easy, but it hasn't been hard either. When I first laid eyes on you, I knew you were the one for me. The way you ride for me and assure me that we can weather any storm. I feel it in my heart that it's time I propose. I'm getting on one knee, will you marry me?" KC revealed. I was ready I know she wasn't expecting this.

"Yes, I will marry you! Where's the preacher?" I said. I started crying. I couldn't believe he actually did it. This night couldn't get any better. I'm glad my parents were in attendance to witness this. This glacier on my finger lit up the room.

"I'm so happy for you congrats," Killany smiled. I'm so proud of those two. She deserves it.

"Thank you! It's been a long time coming," I admitted.

Kaniya

Dro and I made it to Jersey about an hour ago. We booked a room at the Crowne where the party was held. I put the finishing touches on my makeup and messy bun. We were headed to the party. It was actually a nice crowd, I couldn't wait to show my face. I put my twenty-two in my clutch, you never know what could happen. I stopped by the bar and grabbed me a glass of red wine. I headed toward the VIP area to find Killany and her crew. Where's the birthday girl? I walked up in this bitch looking like new money, hand in hand with Dro, I received a lot of lustful stares from the men in VIP. I saw Killany, Raven didn't see me she's too busy in Cartier's face I'll be sure to check her later.

"Baby, I might have to fuck a nigga up for looking at you for too long." Dro snarled. I didn't like how these niggas were openly looking at her like I wasn't with her.

"Calm down let them look, they can't touch. Hey, are you the birthday girl?" I asked. Dro acting crazy already. I finally found Armony.

"I'm here you must be Kaniya, you're gorgeous, is this gift for me?" Armony smiled. I didn't know that she was coming, her husband is fine as fuck.

"It sure is. You look like a princess." I smiled. I caught Armony eye fucking Dro bitch back up before you get fucked up now.

"Hey, Kaniya what are you doing here and where's Tariq?"

Raven snarled. I know she didn't walk up in here with another man and she's engaged to my brother.

"At home. You want to take a picture." I bawled. Raven got an issue it's not the time or place. You can run back and tell whatever, I don't give a fuck. It's always a reason for my actions. Killany and Yung were making their way toward me and that KC guy and Cartier.

"Hey, Kaniya, I missed you! You're carrying my babies good. What's that glow about? Let me find out." Killany admitted. My sister's still fine pregnant and all, a bitch ain't fucking with her. I hate to admit her and Dro do look good together.

"Hey Armony, happy birthday bestie." Menya interrupted. Armony looked flawless, I guess she switched up on the dress because she was slaying tonight. I heard that proposal yuck.

"Hey, Menya long time no see. How you been?" Armony smiled. This bitch really has my dress on that I was supposed to wear. I'm glad Killany told me to do something fresh.

"I've been great; you've made some new friends. Let me introduce you to my new friends." Menya cackled. I motioned with my hands for Toya and Nadia to come over.

"Yo, what the fuck is this Menya? Armony I told you about this bitch," KC snapped. Did this bitch really just bring my ex Nadia in here like that shit was cool.

"Toya, why are you here with your duck ass? Bitch you got my bread?" Yung taunted. I've been looking high and low for this hoe, I let my guard down, and she stole fifty grand from me, and I haven't seen her since.

"I linked up with a bitch, I knew you wouldn't like, you two shared the same nigga. Truth is, I only befriended you because I wanted to fuck your nigga. I offered him the pussy plenty of times. He wouldn't take it. I wondered what was it about me that he wouldn't budge. I hate you, you got everything I want, I coming for everything you got. "Menya spat. The look on this bitches' face was priceless.

"Somebody drop this hoe right where she fucking stands, please." I snarled. I heard too much talking and no fucking action.

"Who the fuck is you?" Menya asked. Nobody had shit to say, but this pregnant chick.

"I'm the bitch that you definitely don't want to see because trust me when I tell you everything you just said you wouldn't have had a chance to say it. Armony it's your birthday, and you're too fucking fly, but dump on this bitch please."I said. The nerve of this backstabbing bitch.

"Trust me, your country ass don't want it," Menya laughed. I pulled out my gun, I hoped they didn't notice what I was doing I was going to kill Armony tonight and kidnap KC.

"Country, I'll let you have that. Armony, cancel this bitch, please. It'll be the best present you could ever give yourself," I insisted. I didn't want to rain on anybody's party, but she needed to get handled quick before I offed her ass.

"I'm too pretty to get my hands dirty today and ruin my party. I hate that you feel that way Menya I really do, but security clear these bitches up out of here. She has gun a and I'll handle her later," Armony smiled. Everything you do in the dark comes to the light. I guess she was a fraud. It was my birthday, and I was surrounded by family I wanted to party and bullshit. I'll address the garbage later.

Killany

Armony's party was finally over. Yung and I said our goodbyes to the crew. We made our way to the car. I couldn't wait to dig in Yung soon as we pulled away from the curb. He never told me about a Toya. I noticed his whole attitude changed after he saw her, he kept stealing glances all night. What you won't do is eye fuck and be disrespectful to me with another bitch while I'm here. I can't hold water I've held it for too long. Who is she?

"Nobody that you need to worry about." Yung snarled. Here she goes with that shit. I knew it was coming.

"Are you sure about that because your eyes were glued to her the whole night?" I sassed. Yung please I never knew him to lie about nothing. It must be something if he's trying to cover shit up.

"Killany, don't start that shit ma, I wasn't even looking that girl," Yung argued. I can tell this is about to be a long night. She can argue with herself, I'm not doing this shit.

"Yung, you are really about to sit her and lie? I've never known you to be a fraud out of all of the months that I've known you," I argued. I'm not even going to say anything else.

"What do I have to lie for Killany? I'm not doing this shit with you. Trust me she doesn't matter if she did you wouldn't be here." Yung said. Killany has no reason to be jealous. Yeah, I had my eyes on Toya the whole night because I had plans to kill her something Killany didn't need to know about. I'll let her think whatever. I need to make sure I get us home safe.

Chapter 30
Killany

Yung and I finally had moved in together despite the little bullshit that transpired a few weeks ago, between us. He purchased us a nice home in Montclair, New Jersey it's in a very nice upscale neighborhood. I've never lived with a man before in all of my twenty-six years of living so this was definitely new and a first for me, but I was adjusting pretty well. Our home had his and hers office space, so I was able to work from home, I was pleased with that. I loved to work more than anything. I need to purchase a fax machine.

Yung was still asleep, so I decided to make him some breakfast which consisted of oatmeal, bacon, cheese eggs, French toast, strawberries, and pineapples. I made fresh orange juice also. Yung should be getting up any minute now. It's really cold in Jersey, I had the heat blasting. Yung and I names were both on the deed. Every morning when I would go run these white folks would look at me like I was crazy, this is a predominantly white neighborhood I would speak because their stares didn't bother me at all. I would always say good morning. It's a nice park in the subdivision I would go there with my laptop and work in the daytime when it warmed up.

This one lady I think her name was Tory she walked up to me and she asked me what do you, and your husband do for a living, your husbands a rapper right and you're a housewife. I politely told her, actually I'm a CPA, and I have my own Payroll firm, and I have the luxury of working from home.

I have a bachelor's degree in accounting. I politely told her to tell me a little bit about you. What do you do? Her mouth dropped when I gave her a rundown of my resume. People are always so quick to judge black people like we are all are rappers and drug dealers, but we aren't we work just as hard as anybody else. That shit pissed me off, don't worry about what we do in our household worry about yourself.

Yung

Killany, must be cooking breakfast this shit smells good, she can cook and fuck like a porn star, and she was smart as hell too. I had the best of both worlds for right now, my mom was dying to meet her. I've never introduced my mom to any female that I've dated before so this would be a first. My mom was dying to meet her because I've never lived with a female before so she was dying to meet Killany. I was going to surprise her today and bring Killany by there, my mom was threating to come by here unannounced. I love my OG to death I was her man since my father died when I was nineteen and I refused to let her date anybody, I shouldn't be selfish but so what it is what is, my sister Megan she couldn't date either fuck that shit too, she was only seventeen anyway.

"Come eat I know you've been up, I need to go and do my morning run. You don't even sleep past eight AM," Killany stated. I started fixing Yung's plate his fat ass could eat, but he worked out religiously, and he was solid muscle.

"I walked up behind Killany while she was cooking and talking shit. I put arms around her waist and grabbed her breast and starting kissing her on her neck that was her spot too. I moved my hands inside of her panty's and that pussy was wet just like I thought, Niagara Falls wet, she should be ashamed of herself." I laughed. It didn't make any sense how wet she was.

"You play too much now I have to change clothes. I hate when you do that. I'm already running late on my workout this morning," Killany mentioned. I hate that my body responded to Yung the way it did. I couldn't change that he had that effect on me, everything with him felt so right.

"What do you have planned today? I wanted you to meet my mom and sister today is that cool with you?" I asked. Killany could be rude and nonchalant. I hope she wouldn't act that way with my OG because I really like her mom and Ray, Kaniya that's a whole different situation.

"You finally want me to meet your mom? What made you change mind all of a sudden? I'm free I don't have much to do but exercise, review a couple of things and then I'm done. "Killany wondered. I wonder what changed Yung's mind. I've been out here in Jersey more than I've been to my own home.

"A lot has changed, you and I changed. I feel it's time or have you changed your mind. "I revealed. I'm trying to eat. Killany always wants a motherfucker to clarify shit for her.

"We changed huh?" Killany laughed. Yung a trip, he basically forced everything. Fuck a flow. He's the only man that I know if he wanted something he was going to get it.

"Hurry up and do your little run and shit and get back to the house so you can meet my OG, my main thang she never disappoints me or gives me any back talk, you could learn a thing or two from her. To be honest, I don't really like you running around out here, we have a built-in gym you need to utilize that. I know you can handle yourself, you swear you're a killer and all but be careful, I would fuck the city up if something happened to you." I warned.

"I'll be careful I promise you, I just like the air it's so crisp, this will be my last time running, I'll just jog in the backyard from now on," Killany stated. Yung really cared about me, and I cared about him also he lived a dangerous life I witnessed that. I will ease up on doing shit that I could've avoided doing, anybody could get touched even me. I would listen to what he was saying.

Chapter 31

Killany

It was a little after nine a.m., and the birds were chirping the air was crisp but not as crisp like It would've been an hour ago. I was only going to run for about forty-five minutes, I wanted some dope dick, and I needed a deep death stroke, When Yung put in work he snatches a bitches' soul, I'm an angel and sex with him is a brief encounter with the devil. It's amazing, that's the best sex I've ever had. I need some before I meet Yung's mom, that would be an even better work out. I needed a smile etched on my face. Just thinking about it, let me run my ass back home. I finally made it back to the house, I noticed the mailman just ran I was about to check the mail, something was off, my front door was wide opened. I grabbed my gun from the nape of my back and pulled the other one out of my shoe. I made my way up the driveway and toward the door, nothing looks out of place, I went to the hall closet and grabbed the Ak-47 because if a mother fucker was in here unexpected, it was lights off up in this bitch, trust me they will meet their creator. I put on my bullet proof vest on also, I made my way to the bedroom I took the stairs two at a time, I heard some action Yung was getting robbed, man what the fuck is going on, nobody knew where we lived. If they were looking for money and work he didn't keep that shit here, my room was a fucking mess. It was six niggas on him they had my baby hog tied, he wasn't giving up, though. I have to execute this shit well, I made a loud noise so they could send somebody to come and check it out the first dummy came and I lit his bitch ass up. I was off in the corner where nobody could see where the shots were coming from, two more came down the stairs running.

I lit their ass up; one headshot and one shot in the chest. Three down and three to go, two more men came down the stairs just shooting, it was funny because they didn't see me as soon as he made to the seventh step I lit his ass up. Thank God for this ninety-round drum, the other guy ran down the steps like he was about to come and find me I put the scope on and shot him dead in his eye his head exploded. Five were dead, the last guy was begging Yung to tell him where the work was, he had his back turned. I used my thirty-eight on him, I shot him in his back, and he fell to the floor. I walked up on him, and shot him in his knee. I untied Yung and left him alive so he could question this pussy.

Yung

Killany, give me a kiss baby, I love you more than you will ever know. I appreciate you for what you just did for me, promise me you'll never leave me. If I never believed in God before or angels, I know God had to create Killany for me. I was hemmed up by six niggas and today could've been my expiration date, my baby laid every last one of these niggas down by her fucking self, she listened to me this time and left one alive. Killany is one woman that can never leave me, she was the one for me, I planned on marrying her. Pussy, who sent you, Killany grab that niggas phone.

"I will never tell, kill me now pussy. Your bitch got a lot of heart." Algieri spat.

"Killing you is too easy, I'll make you suffer motherfucker," I yelled. I didn't have any beef with Jamaicans, the fuck they trying to get at me for.

"His phone is clean, but I know a hacker who can get in this shit and see what's up," Killany said. Somebody had it out for Yung, I can't believe he said he loved me that's a first. I guess shit has changed. He kissed me like it was going to be his last time, I'm glad I came back home to get some of that dope dick. I was right on time, that's crazy. I needed to listen to Yung more because if I would've stayed at home, this would've never happened. I would've met these niggas at the front door, my man is still breathing so it what it is.

"Call KC, and I'm about to hit up the clean-up crew, check their pockets for phones and ID when you came through did you see any vehicles that you've never seen before they didn't get here on foot where did they park," I demanded. This shit isn't adding up at all. This happened too quick.

KC

Yung called me and stated rock a bye baby, get here quick. This is the third fucking time some shit popped off. I don't know what the fuck is going on, first the warehouse shit, then me and Armony in New York, now this we were caught off guard the whole time. Yung just moved in this house about a month ago. Nobody knew where he lived. I lived about thirty minutes away. I was trying to be there in fifteen minutes. We were about to meet with a new connect in a few weeks, and this was definitely bad for business. I thought shit was going good, but damn every corner I turn it's some bullshit going. I finally made it over to Yung's house everything looked in place. I hopped out and made my way in, you have to move different in the suburbs, you never know whose watching. I made my way to the back door. I couldn't go through the front; I didn't need anybody getting a glimpse of any bodies lying around. I let myself in because I had a key. Yung where you at.

"I'm in the family room." Yung blurted. KC finally made it over here.

"What the fuck is this? What happened? Killany you good, damn this is a fucking massacre." I asked. How did Killany pull all of this shit off by herself? These niggas look real familiar I can't think of where I knew them from.

"I was just about to take a shower, I don't know how they got in, I heard a noise when I came out to see what was going on they yanked me out of the shower demanding drugs and money," Yung stated. Nobody knew where the fuck I lived not even my OG. I'm glad Killany was here, but damn I didn't want her exposed to all of this shit, hands down she can handle it but since she's met me her whole life has changed because of me. She's been dropping bodies like it's a fucking hobby. I've exposed her too much shit already and got her caught up in bullshit since she's met me. I'm supposed to protect her, it shouldn't be the other way around.

"I'm good KC, but forget all of that. Here's the phones and they all have one number in common it's a local number. Look maybe you guys and can find out whose number this is." Killany suggested. I gave the phones to Yung and KC so they could see.

"Killany, pack you a bag and go to my house with Armony. Yung, do you see whose jack this is?" I revealed. I don't know if Yung recognized the numbers, but I fucking did. Why would they be trying to take us out?

"You have to be fucking kidding me, why would he have a hit out on me? This shit is blowing my fucking mind." Yung thought to himself. I knew them fuck niggas was moving funny. KC didn't want to believe that shit. I understood where he was coming from. The key word was Jamaicans each encounter. We didn't have any beef with Jamaicans. This shit is very personal.

Armony

KC called me about fifteen minutes ago, and told me to be looking out for Killany she was on her way some shit just popped off and meet her at the front door. If it's not one thing, it's something else. We can't catch a fucking break it's ridiculous. Yung and Killany stayed about thirty minutes from us they should be here in no time. I can only imagine what happened, It has to be serious if KC rushed out of the house to see what transpired. I just want my happy and peace of mind back if only for a month. That'll be too much like right. My doorbell rang breaking me out of my thoughts that must be Killany.

"Girl, let me in. I need some tea and some clothes to change in." Killany said. This life we live is crazy, but I won't let that get me down.

"Follow me, what happened." I blurted out. Killany still has her bullet proof vest on and work out attire.

"Somebody broke in the house and tried to rob Yung, I'm not for sure if they were going to kill him. I wasn't taking any chances. It was some more fucking Jamaicans. I went to go run for about a little while. I changed my mind because I wanted some dick and headed back to the house. The front door was open, and I heard some noise coming from upstairs I took a peek, and it was going down. I had to get them up off of Yung because I wasn't fucking losing him. I killed five people today. To make matters worse we're supposed to head to Atlanta tomorrow they have that meeting." Killany confessed. All of this shit happens the day before.

"It'll be alright we'll get through this like we've gotten through everything else. I'm sure you'll be staying here tonight. No matter what happens today trust me KC and Yung aren't canceling whatever business they have in Atlanta." I assured her. Killany and I have found ourselves in some tough position these past few months. I pray everything works out fine.

Chapter 32

KC

Yung and I had a meeting with a possible new connect. It was a supplier down South that was operated and owned by a duo; Black and his partner Abel, they were from Atlanta. They had the South sewed up and a lot of the Tristate area. Their names rang bells in the underworld. I heard of them, I couldn't really confirm if we were doing business or not. Yung and I had to feel their vibe to make sure they weren't informants. This deal has been in the works for a couple of weeks now. We had to tie up some loose ends before we decided to check out this distributor. Our old connect was moving a little funny. The product was still good, the prices were good, but It was time for us to venture out and try some different options and a new product.

Our flight was set to leave at noon. We would land in Atlanta after three PM. I was actually flying domestic this time. I was moving different, and so were people around me. The only people that I trusted where Yung, Cartier, and Armony. My dad has ears everywhere, I guess he heard that I was looking for a new connect and he forbid me to have this meeting. I was a grown ass man, and I do what the fuck I want. That's the main reason why I wasn't taking my private jet. My dad keeps his plane chartered there also, and I didn't trust him, so that's why I was flying Delta. Something just seemed off about him, he had eyes on me, and I had eyes on him too. Time would tell, everything you do in the dark comes to the light.

Yung

I was getting my duffle bag packed. We had a meeting with a possible new connect tomorrow in Atlanta. Killany wanted to come with me to see her family. I wasn't against it, but I couldn't let her fly with me because I was flying Delta Airlines and you never know who's watching. The line of work I'm in is complicated, and the Feds are always watching. I don't need Killany to get jammed or caught up fucking with me and the shit that I have going on. Conspiracy is a hard case to beat, and I don't need anybody thinking she knows shit about me and she doesn't, so her and Armony flew out yesterday together. I had a good feeling about this new venture. I think it would work out fine, our old connect wanted us out for some reason that shit doesn't sit right with me.

I was moving with caution, KC was my charger partner we move on one accord, but when the time was right I was going to cut off the connects air supply whether or not KC gave me the go. I don't care, nobody can get at me and live to tell about it unless I'm six feet deep and as you can see I'm still breathing. I keep my eyes open and my ears to the street. I moved my OG out of the city because if something happened to her, all bets were fucking off. I had some shit in the works. I put Cartier up on game, so he could be aware of his surroundings. I knew he could take care of himself, but I needed him to be on point at all times.

Cartier

KC and Yung went to Atlanta for the weekend to check out some new business ventures. I stayed behind to keep an eye on things. KC and Yung thought I was green to a lot of shit, but I'm an observer. I sit back and peep shit out. I was sitting at the warehouse like I normally do. I don't trust nobody overseeing my money but me. After the little run in they had a month ago. I had security in this bitch airtight. The inside was deeply secured, and I had the outside secured within an eight-hundred-foot radius nothing was moving in here and out of here that I didn't know about.

A lot of the people that worked here used to work for our old connect. As of right now the connect has in issue with us. So, guess who was the first motherfuckers to go; his people. Their loyalty will always be with them and not with us, so I cut ties and switched up our operation and put those cowards to sleep. I didn't need them running back telling how we moved our shit. Every surveillance system that was in here I replaced it all. My system was tighter than the fucking white house. Everything has been running a lot smoother since I got rid of the dead weight. I couldn't understand why Taliyae was lurking, our security spotted him and his men outside snooping around. Uncle's friend or not nigga you trespassing on private property you can get these slugs too. I hit KC and Yung and told them what was happening, once they hit me back giving me the ok it was a done deal.

Kanan(Abel)

Black set up a meeting with KC and Yung they were looking for a new connect. We were looking to expand in Jersey. I was coming for everything that Alibumbiyae took from me including my son. What's so crazy about this situation is Alibumbiyae was KC and Yung's connect. I had to find my son and know everything about him. I've been watching him for about two months now. It fucks with me that I was denied the chance to be in his life. He wanted to be my son's father so fucking bad, but you're taxing the fuck out of him. You've been setting him up so his empire would crumble because you know that I'm coming for your ass. If KC and I established a relationship I would politely give him my shit and retire, I owed him that much.

A lot of shit was going on, and Killany was smack dead in the middle of it, and another female who I assumed was KC's girlfriend. The two of them have been doing some hot ass shit. Killian would shit bricks if he knew Killany was dropping bodies every time she blinks an eye. I don't even know how to approach KC about this, of course, I was going to be his connect. I've been watching him for months, and he moves just like me. I haven't told Sonja shit because he knew had a mother and he probably thinks that she didn't give a fuck about him. But, he knows that he has a father, but Alibumbiyae wasn't him. The meeting was scheduled to happen in about two hours I had a lot of shit on my mind.

"Kanan, how do you want to do this shit man, what's the plan?

What the fuck you need me to do besides talk and observe?" Black asked. We finally found my nephew and nobody was about to stop this reunion, not even Alibumbiyae.

"Man, I don't know I have to feel his vibe first, but he will know that he's my fucking son today," I revealed. It's been a long time coming. KC looks just like me, when I look at him, I see Sonja and me.

"Straight like that huh?" Black asked. What if he decides not to do business with us? That's a possibility with all of this shit coming out. We're not looking to gain anything. He can have this empire, it's rightfully his since he's the oldest son.

"Hell yeah. I've already lost twenty-eight years I'm not losing shit else. Not doing business with us is not an option." I revealed. He might be mad at first, but he'll get over it. This shit personal for me. I got something for Ali, he played a dangerous game.

"What about Sonja?" Black questioned. I think she should get to meet her son.

"What about her she didn't tell me shit until three months ago, should I tell her? "I asked. Fuck ass no. Sneaky ass never thought about telling me until she got caught.

"I think you should. "Black suggested. She should get the chance to meet him, but not today.

"I don't want her to meet him on my time. You better not tell Chelle," I warned. If I keep this shit to myself. I'm no better than her. I'm real about what I do, I'll let Sonja know afterward. Not before.

Alimbumbiyae

I'm sure y'all have heard about me. I'm here now in the flesh believe half of what you hear and go off what you see. I'm a monster, and I do what the fuck I want and not what I can. I hate that it has to come to this, but I can't, and I won't let KC meet with his father and Black. I knew what I did was wrong so what. I've raised him as my own since he was born I'm all he knows, and nobody was going to take that from me, not even the bitch and nigga that created him. I knew all about KC and Yung looking for a new connect, that was cool with me I'm never worried about who goes. I'm worried about who stays.

When I found out, the new connect was Black and his father all bets were fucking off. This shit was not about to happen. KC must have felt something was off because he didn't use his personal plane he flew domestic, that was cool but I had plans to intercept that shit. I was making my way to Atlanta as we speak and snatching him and Yung both up. I needed to explain some things to KC but not everything. Abel or Kanan thought he was invisible anybody could get touched fucking with me and Black too, I had Couture on standby. I wish I could kill my sister Amber for putting KC's birth certificate on Kanan's windshield. None of this would've ever happened. I have eyes on Sonja she should've stopped this shit. If things go left, she'll be the first one dead, KC will never meet his mammy.

Abel(Kanan)

Boys do what they can, and men do what they want. Atlanta is my city, and I'm aware of everything that's going and coming. KC's flight was about to arrive in about forty-five minutes. I received a call that Alibumbiyae just touched down in my city on my turf. I'm sure he knew that I was about to be my son's connect whether he liked it or not that shit was about to happen. You wanted to play God and dictate shit in my life well today you will meet the fucking devil because I'm coming. I had my task force all throughout Hartsville-Jackson Airport, as soon as he made a move on KC and Yung I was setting it off in this bitch today. I was making a fucking mess after I finished Ali was dying today. I don't know why Sonja kept calling my phone today. I thought about it I'm going to let her meet KC, but not today.

"You straight over there?" Black asked. Shit was about to get real within an hour. I was ready to get sideways.

"I'm good I can't wait to torture this goat eating motherfucker." I snarled. I can't believe he did all of this behind some pussy that didn't want him. I've been waiting for this day for months. I can feel It.

KC

My flight just landed in Atlanta I have a funny feeling some shit was about to go down. The storm was coming today I could feel it. I grabbed my carry on. I had some luggage to pick up. My straps were in there. Armony and Killany should be out here already to pick us up. I tapped Yung because he fell asleep.

"KC, why did you let me fall asleep? Nigga we made it." Yung boasted. Once this merger was finalized, I planned on celebrating. I've been wanting this merger to happen for over a month now. Killany and I were headed to Jamaica for three weeks.

"Yeah, we made it, I need you on go mode some shit doesn't feel right. I don't know what it is now, but I'm sure I'll find out later it'll be revealed. I trust my instincts; some shit was about to happen it can either make me or break me. Whatever I endured today, I prayed for the lost souls, they will feel my wrath forcefully. We made our way off the plane. We were headed toward our luggage. I knew some shit was off, my father was standing by our gate waiting on us. I nudged Yung so he could look up and see what caught my attention." I warned.

"The fuck his pussy ass doing here?" Yung snarled. If he thought that he was about to stop what the fuck we had going on he was sadly mistaken. This fuck nigga has been fucking us for months, and I haven't got at him yet on the strength of KC because we move together. He started walking towards us with his crew. I didn't want to be too loud because the airport was busy and people were looking at us. The shit looked suspect.

"What's up? You two don't look happy to see me?" Alibumbiyae admitted. KC knew what time it was. I was killing any competition, I'll match whatever and give extra for the same price this shit wasn't happening today. I didn't want to get ignorant because the airport was full and police were everywhere.

"You good, I wasn't expecting to see you here, how long will you be here, you want to hit the strip club tonight?" I asked. I knew exactly what he was trying to do, but that shit wasn't about to be ok with me. He brought his whack ass crew, it's a shame what a nigga will do behind some paper.

"I didn't come here for that, I'm a businessman, I have an offer that you can't refuse, and I won't let you decline it, come with me. Grab their things. "Alibumbiyae boasted. KC was starting to act like his mammy and disobey what the fuck I said. I don't tolerate that shit at all not from him or nobody else.

"I'm good you came all the way here to make me an offer that I can't refuse? I'll hit you up when I get back home, and we can talk." I said. This man is up to some shit. I couldn't wait to find out what he was up to.

"If it isn't the infamous Alibumbiyae, it's been a long time coming. "Kanan snarled and clapped his hands together. This fuck nigga was really trying to stop me from meeting my son. I signaled for my task force to grab his crew and usher them toward the tunnel I don't need this shit on camera.

"Abel, that's your name right long time no see. You used to

work for me. "Alimbumbiyae voice boomed. Where in the fuck did, this nigga come from? I thought I was two steps ahead of this nigga, but it looks like I'm two steps behind him and outnumbered.

"Call me Kanan, pussy. What's up KC What's up Yung? Black, look after my precious cargo.

Ali, bitch you know what fucking time it is," Kanan snarled. I couldn't wait to snap his fucking neck.

"Hell nah, I remember this old nigga from the barbecue we went to in the summer time he was acting a fool behind some woman. It's a small world." I thought to myself.

"Hell nah, that's Killany's uncle Kanan I remember him from the cook-out when he came in acting crazy, and we watched his ass to see how he moved." Yung I thought to myself. What beef does he have with Ali?

Armony

Killany and I were meeting KC and Yung at the airport we have been waiting for over thirty minutes for them to come out. Something didn't feel right we parked the SUV and headed toward the gate. I couldn't bring any guns in here, but I knew for a fact KC and Yung had some in their luggage so if need be we could get to them.

"Trust me Yung and KC are good; I'm not feeling a bad vibe, but we'll see once we make it toward the gate." Killany disclosed. I tried to think positive and not negative, but here lately shit has been going south so anything could happen.

"I'll take your word for it, we made it through security pretty quick." I smiled. KC and I are in sync with one another, and something is wrong he would've been out here he hates airports.

"There they are what are they doing with my uncles Kanan and Black? "Killany revealed. What the fuck is really going, what's Kanan doing here? I ran toward Yung and Armony ran toward KC. This view before us didn't look too good. I grabbed that suitcase quick as fuck. It looked like I would be needing it soon.

"Wait a minute Killany you know those two," I whispered. What's really going on? Killany's uncle was about to reveal some shit, and I'm all ears. Ali looks like he was deer about to be caught in headlights.

Chapter 33

Killany

I'm so tired of this back and forth shit with Yung it's ridiculous. Ever since we came back from Atlanta a few days ago. He's been acting real funny. I don't know what happened out there. I never got the full story. I take that back I noticed the change after Armony's party when his ex-Toya showed up. He hasn't even been coming home like he should. He leaves before I wake up and comes back after I'm sleeping. One minute he says that he doesn't think that I'm a fit for this lifestyle and I proved to him on more than one occasion I'm built for this shit and he just gives me his ass to kiss, and I'm tired of it. Before I make permanent decisions on temporary emotions, I'm going to call my mother she's my voice of reason. Something's telling me I really need to leave Yung and fuck riding for him and proving to him how down I am. He ain't proved shit to me.

"Killany Denise, what? You want a child?" Kaisha asked. I'm not used to Killany calling me every day.

"Ma I'm leaving Yung I can't do this shit no more. It's not working for me. I can't be with somebody who can only give me half of him," I pleaded. I had to get my mom's opinion on this one.

"Killany Denise do you love Yung? If you do, then you need to fight for that shit because you're stubborn and he's stubborn. Why do you want to leave him? What did he do?" Kaisha asked. I needed to know what did he do for Killany to consult with me before she left him. Killany and Yung were destined to be, the two of them remind me of Killian and I when we first started out.

"Ma I do love him. I can't lie but I love myself more, and I will not tolerate any more of Yung's shit. I'm woman enough to walk away and say fuck it. It's too much and a lot of shit that I can't say over the phone that's a conversation we'll have face to face," I revealed. I'm fed up, and I 've had enough, I'm good on him. I don't care what type of boss or savage he is, fuck him it's all about me.

"Killany baby listen to me. Loving a savage and a boss ain't easy. You may endure some things that you don't like, and you don't agree with. Does he put his hands on you? Is he cheating? He may be going through some things that he doesn't know how to cope with. One of the hardest things I've ever done was walk away from the love of my life. Fight Killany, don't walk away, don't make permanent decisions on temporary emotions you have to go through this to get to where you're going, " Kaisha coaxed. I hope Killany is listening to me, she's so stubborn and headstrong. She gets that from me too, I don't want her running when stuff doesn't go her way.

"No ma he doesn't hit me, and he's not cheating on me. I don't want to fight for him I've fought enough. I'm not you, and I'm damn sure not Kaniya it's easier for me to say fuck Yung and move on. I love myself way more than to tolerate a man who constantly throws shit up in my face that I don't fit in with his lifestyle, so I'll gracefully bow out." I interrupted. I can't take it anymore I'm not happy, my life was good before Yung and will be great after Yung.

"I hear you, baby, are you going home or you're coming to Georgia," Kaisha asked. Killany is serious she is fed up with Yung.

"I'm going home to my house, my bags are already packed, and I left Yung two letters one on the nightstand and one on the refrigerator, I'm gone. I'll see him when I see him." I said. I'm done it's not worth it, I won't lose myself over him.

"You going somewhere Killany?" Yung said. I heard Killany's whole conversation I've been standing here for about twenty minutes listening. She's running her mouth and telling somebody she's about to leave me. Try and die the moment she let me between her legs and put that pussy on me it was a wrap, ain't no breaking up.

"I'm leaving you, Yung, it's a wrap have a nice life. I can't do this thing with you anymore." I warned him. Speak of the devil he walked in when I was leaving out.

"Why you leaving Killany? You finally realized you ain't built for this life? You thought you were you going to leave me and not say shit?" Yung argued. I love Killany, but I'm not going to pacify her and pat her on the back and tell her she's doing great all the time. Tough love is the best love. She's my rider, I have never met a female like Killany, but if I ease up on her, she loses focus. I'm a man with a lot of enemies and niggas will gun for Killany because they can't get to me, so I need her on go at all times.

"Yes, that why I'm leaving I'm not built for this shit or you. You hit it right on the nose it was nice knowing you. I'll see you when I see you. I actually left you a note explaining why I'm leaving, but I'm always a woman about mine so I can tell you face to face."I admitted. This is by far the hardest thing that I've ever had to do in life is walk away from the love of my life, but it is what is. He can't talk to me any kind of way, and that's why he's going to learn the hard way.

Hey ma, that's what you want? You leaving me it's a wrap straight like that? You fold under pressure ma. You leaving nigga over some petty shit. I thought you was different Killany," Yung said. I can see it in her eyes that she doesn't want to leave me, but her pride is a motherfucker, and she wants to feel like she's doing something. My pride a motherfucker too, but I love her, and I need her she's the only thing that keeps me sane. I need to let her know how I feel about her because tomorrow isn't promised to a savage like me.

"Yes, this is what I want I've made my mind up. I'm not leaving you about nothing petty Yung. I love you I can't lie but I love myself more and here lately you've been giving me nothing but your ass to kiss. I'm here in Jersey all alone. Armony she's straight, but I didn't move here for her, I moved here for you. The way you talk to me and call yourself handling me I can't deal with that." I admitted. I laid my feelings out there.

"On some real shit Killany, I've never loved a chick how I love you. I know this shit is new to you, but it's new to me also. Let a nigga love you the right way, though. Tough love is the best love, I'm a savage out here in these streets. I step on toes daily, but I have to be that way with you because people will get at you to get to me. I refuse to let you walk out of my life because of shit that I say to you that you don't like. I love you ma I need you to keep riding for me like you've been doing?" Yung revealed. I put it out there, I felt Killany needed to hear that.

"Yung, do you hear that?" I asked. Somebody's outside I peeped out the window and saw the Feds they have this bitch swarmed.

"It's the Feds they have the house surrounded. I got to dip ma I don't know what they about to hit a nigga with. The house is clean no guns or dope you should be good, but I got to bail. You were built for this you know what do. You know where all of my money is here's my black card and shit I'm going to leave this phone here. Hit Cartier and KC when they leave, I'll get up with you." Yung said. Damn a nigga in some heavy shit if the Feds about to kick this bitch in. My lawyers haven't given me the heads up on no pending cases I have to trash this cell phone and get up of out of here this bitch could be tapped.

"I love you Yung, be safe. I got this," I said. Damn this shit crazy.

"Open up! Open up! Before we forcefully come in. We have a warrant for the arrest of Killany Denise Miller for the murder of an FBI agent you have the right to remain silent anything you say can be used against you in the court of law." FBI officer stated.

"What the fuck? Murder me, how did I get caught up on a murder charge? I was about to leave, I thought they were looking for Yung they're looking for me? Let me call Ma and Daddy.

"Killany Denise what child?" Kaisha asked. I hope she changed her mind about leaving Yung.

"Ma the Feds are here at Yung's house they got a warrant for my arrest on a murder charge call daddy on three way I haven't let them in yet," I said. I can't believe this shit.

"Yeah baby what's up?" Killan asked. I put my sexy voice on for Kaisha.

"Daddy it's me the Feds are outside of Yung's house they have an arrest warrant for me on a murder charge," I admitted. I hated to tell him this, but I had too.

"Killany go out there and comply. Do what they tell you to do. I'll be there in three hours, keep your phone on speaker so I can hear everything. Don't worry baby, daddy got you. I'll be there in a minute," Killan vowed. I can't believe my baby got jammed up on some bullshit. It's cool though she'll be out I know some people. Money talk and bullshit walks a thousand miles.

"Killany Denise baby I love you, and I'm on my way. Momma will see you in a minute keep your head up baby girl and don't fold. Pressure bust pipe. We apply pressure. Don't say shit about nothing. I know some of the best attorneys in the area you'll be out in no time. I know this is a big mistake, but I'll get this shit squared away trust me." Kaisha boasted. Whoever got my daughter jammed up on some bullshit will have to see me about this shit. I don't play about mine at all.

"I'm a big girl I can handle this let me go face the music and open the door and get this shit on the road," I admitted. Loving a savage ain't easy.

Put your hands up. Any weapons Ms.? Spread them. Where're the guns, drugs? You're going to be gone for a long time since you killed an FBI agent. I'm taking the whole Miller Family down one by one starting with you.

The End... For Now

Contest Alert for Your Chance to win. The first place winner
will win a Kindle Fire!

Three 20.00 Amazon Gift Cards will be gifted also.

Email entry's to authoressnikkinicole@gmail.com book
must be read and reviewed to qualify.

1.   When did Yung and Killany first meet?

2.   What triggered Yung to come to Atlanta to stop
Killany in her tracks.

3.   How old Is Armony?

4.   Armony and Killany caught bodies together
how many and where?

5.   Who are KC's parents?

6.   Why did Killany leave Yung?

Sneak Peek of Baby I Play for Keeps 3

Baby, I'm Still Playing for Keeps

Written by: Nikki Nicole

Sonja

I can't believe Kanan has found out about our son. The only people that knew about our son were Kaisha and Chelle. That's one secret that we all agreed that we were taking to our grave. They didn't even have access to our son's birth certificate. It peeks my interest to know where he got that birth certificate from. I knew for a fact they wouldn't place this shit in Kanan's face. I had that information secured at the Bank of America on Peachtree St. Downtown Atlanta in my safe deposit box. I had to fake like I was dead. Thank God he didn't check for my pulse. He wasn't gone yet I could still hear him and the twins talking, and I still heard footsteps.

"I'm going to call the clean-up crew, and I'll be back. Ride with me Yashir and Kanan Jr." Kanan, I knew Sonja wasn't dead because I didn't choke her ass out like that. I just applied some pressure to her neck. I got something for her ass. As soon as she thinks she's about to tiptoe around this bitch and disappear, I'm going to snatch her ass up. I need some answers.

"Saved by the clean-up crew I have to get the hell up out of here. Before Kanan comes back. I'm not taking shit with me, but my phone and my wallet, I needed to blow this joint." Sonja, I could speak about this shit because no one was here but me. Hopefully, the good Lord himself would hear my cry's. Why is my life so complicated? I never thought this secret would come out. That's one of the reasons why I didn't want to raise nobody else's damn kids because a nigga took my one and only from me because I didn't choose him over my son's father.

"Going somewhere bitch? You thought I was gone huh? Enlighten me on that shit that you were just spitting. Who took our son? How come you never told me about this shit? "Kanan asked. Why would she keep something like this from me? She had an affair on me I can't believe this shit.

Where should I start?" Sonja said. Damn, I really didn't want to have to explain this shit to Kanan. I see I don't have a choice now.

"Start from the fucking beginning. Explain to me how you and Ali Bum Biyae had an affair and don't leave shit out." Kanan, if I've never prayed before in my life, I prayed today that Lord help me get through this. I understood the whole Deuce situation because of the circumstances, but to have my child and never mention anything to me about it. Not to mention you had an affair with Ali Bum Biyae. Two wrongs don't make a right, but damn did you have to get a nigga back like that.

"Do I really have to explain this situation detail for detail?" Sonja asked. I'm a woman about mine first and foremost. I can own up to anything and everything that I've done. I really don't want to explain this scandal to Kanan how I had an affair with his connect Ali Bum Biyae.

Even though I knew Ali Bum Biyae before him. He has never explained shit to me about the affairs that he had.

"Yes, Sonja I want to know detail for detail. I promise you I won't get mad or put my hands on you again. I just want to know where can I find my son and the reason that he was taken from us.

Why didn't you tell me that you were pregnant?" Kanan, men lie, and women lie. A woman has the power to make you or break you down in the worse way possible.

I have a son that twenty-eight years old that means that Sonja cheated on me in the beginning way before Yasmine was ever introduced in the picture. Don't get me wrong I've done my share of shit. I used to entertain females here and there and have casual sex, but this shit here is fucking with my mental and emotions.

"Let me say this Kanan I knew Ali Bum Biyae way before you, and I ever met. My mother used to cook up work for his father. His brother Taliyae Bum Biyae is Tariq's father. Our affair first started when you started copping more weight from him. Lloyd and Ike got pulled by the police, and you decided to send me, Kaisha, and Chelle to go instead because the chances of us getting pulled were slim to none. It started out as casual flirting you started becoming really heavy in the streets more than you already were. You paid me little to no attention and entertaining more hoes. At this time, we were just talking on the phone.

I don't know if you remember the trip that Ali Bum Biyae requested you, Killian, and Black to come to Atlantic City and you advised to me that he never showed, yet instead you met with his father and the pill connect. We hooked up that weekend, he sent you guys away so that we could hook-up. We ended up having sex that weekend. We snuck around for a couple of months. I was pregnant before he and I had sex. I stopped seeing him because I was pregnant. He took our child because I refused to leave you and be with him. He threatened to kill you. It got so bad I don't know if you remember when the spots kept getting raided and someone stole a million from us, you never found out who that was, it was him. He threatened to kill your mom if I ever spoke on this shit. That's why you never knew he took our son, so he would always have a piece of me." Sonja said. She just laid it all out there.

"He did all of this shit to me because you cut the pussy off? He took my son from me. He took a million dollars from me. He threatened to kill my momma and me. He got my traps hit up. He wanted a piece of you. You mean he wanted to deprive me to know my son and you to be a mother to him because he couldn't have you? He's Tariq's uncle? He's started a war. I'm going to take everything from him since he's taken so much from me. I need you in on this. I wish you would've told me, because I would've rocked his ass to sleep years ago, if he would've come for me.

Why didn't you tell me? How can you live with yourself knowing you have a son out there? Have you ever looked for him? How did you hide your pregnancy? Who was there with you when you delivered? Where in the fuck can I find him?" Kanan asked. I can't even stand in the same room with Sonja after all out of this shit she just put out there. I have a Jr. who doesn't even know me because a man wanted to play God and dictate my life how he sees fit.

"Yes, he killed my fucking mother, I think he killed Tyra too. Taliyae is Tariq's father. Kaisha and Chelle were there with me.

We tried to escape because we knew his intentions. He had the hospital on lock. Yes, I looked for my son day in and day out. I didn't hide my pregnancy because I was so pissed with you I would lay with my back turned against you and you were never home. Remember your attention wasn't on me, your money started to pile up and so did the hoes, so you were never home." I'm so pissed he's opening up old wounds. I've been through so much in my life that people don't even know about. Thank God I don't look like what I've been through, all of these questions that he's throwing at me I can't deal with it. I'm at my fucking breaking point I can fucking explode.

"Let me call Kanan and Black up. Kill where's your fucking wife at?

"I don't fucking know. Call her your damn self," Killian said. Why is he calling my phone looking for Kaisha?

"Pull up over to Sonja's house right now," Kanan said. I need you right now, some shit just popped off.

"Sonja, call Kaisha and tell her to bring her ass over here now," Kanan, I needed her in on this shit also.

"Yo, Black where you at? I need you on the track, bring Chelle with you and some heat just come to play." Kanan, Black is ready for some action.

Kaniya

Work Now Atlanta is finally open for business and I have fifty people staffed and hired for full-time work, and new people are registering every day, that's a blessing. I promise you I thought this day would never come. I've been putting all of my energy into this. A lot of new shops have opened up in this retail space; a shoe store was opening up next to me on the right. I haven't met the owner yet, and to the left of me a new coffee shop has opened up I met the owner Dacent, she was pretty nice.

Raven was working as the receptionist for me until she started school that worked out perfect.

"Kaniya, you have some more roses this time he sent white and black." Raven ugh Lucky gets on my fucking nerves what's the meaning of all of this, he interrupted my FaceTime with Cartier for this bullshit.

"Ray, really well he sends them every day. I haven't heard from him. I appreciate the decor." Kaniya said. Lucky doesn't scare me with black roses every day do what you have to do. Damn who is this fine ass man coming through my place of business.

"Is the owner available," Dro asked. Damn it sure is a lot of black roses in here she must have pissed some man off he's at the point where he wants to kill her that's what black roses mean.

"Who wants to know? Do you have an appointment?" Raven

what does this fine ass man want. I can tell by the way Kaniya's looking at him that she likes what she sees, my sister is a fucking mess, that's why she has so much drama going on now.

"Look shawty, I need to speak with the owner now. Damn, can you get her out here for me or do I need to go in the back and get her." Dro, shawty was working my last nerves.

"I'm the owner how can I help you," Kaniya said. What the fuck does he want?

"What's hannin' shawty, I'm Dro. I own the shoe store next door, I wanted to know if you can find me some people to work for me," Dro said. Damn shawty bad, too bad she knocked up already.

"Oh ok partner, I'm Kaniya you can visit my website and schedule an appointment so I can know your preferences. "Kaniya said. I don't know who he thinks he is barging in my office thinking he running shit.

"Look shawty I don't have time to do that shit. I don't do the internet shit, my assistant does and she ain't fucking working today. Let me put some money in your pockets, help a nigga out, damn," Dro said. I see what type of female she is, but she thinks she's running shit and likes to have control. Meanwhile, her lil' stunts she's playing got my dick brick hard.

"Let me explain something to you, Dro. I don't know how you run your business, but I handle things different at Work Now Atlanta. I do things with protocol and the only reason I'm considering helping you today because you've made a scene at my place of business. Follow me to my office Dro." Kaniya said. I can already tell I don't like his fine ass. I had to put a little pep in my step I know he's watching me.

"Shawty, you don't have to do all of that shit," Dro said. Her young ass will fuck around and get this dick put in her with that walk, I'm trying to spare her.

"My name is Kaniya, but you can call me Ms. Miller if you don't like it, don't look that's just the way I walk I'm sorry. You can have a seat here, and we can get straight to business." Kaniya said. Got him, I should stop being a tease, but oh well it's fun damn right I got it.

"Some nigga want to murk you, huh?" Dro asked. I had to ask her that.

"Not that I know of why do you ask?" Kaniya said. We are supposed to be talking about finding him some staff, not me.

"You know what you do steal some paper or some work?" Dro asked. I'm getting all in shawty's personal shit because if something pops off I'm right next door. Obviously, they know where she works, and they haven't made a move yet.

"Why are you worried about someone that you don't know? I didn't steal no paper or no work. I was with a man for six years, cheated on me and I found out. I left him, we had sex the same day, and I had a get back fling the next day and I'm pregnant with twins, and he may not be the father, so he's in his feeling. That's why you see black roses through this building anything else you want to know or can get back to business," Kaniya said. I just gave his ass a mouth full.

"Oh ok, I'll call you Mrs. Shannon I'll take care of you and your two kids," Dro said. I had to throw that out there to see what her response would be.

"I don't mix business with pleasure, but let's get to business though here's the paperwork fill it out so I can know exactly what you're looking for," Kaniya said. Lord, please get this man up out of my office. He's coming on too strong. I'll come up out this skirt and put this pussy on him. He'll be another stalker on my list.

"I feel you shawty, let me take you to lunch or something, and we discuss this paperwork further, and I'll have my assistant meet us there to fill it out. I'm not taking no for an answer bring your ass on." Dro said. Damn, I want shawty in the worst way. I love her slick ass mouthpiece she got on her, but she got some baggage too. I don't know if I can deal with that.

"I have plans already for lunch. I brought my lunch thank you for the offer you can get started on your paperwork so we can get finished." Kaniya said. Who's pranking me right now with this guy?

"Ray, where's Kaniya tell her I'm out here," Lucky asked. She got me fucked up I heard that fuck nigga tried to push up on her.

"She's with a potential client Lucky you have to come back or sit up here in the Lobby and wait," Raven said. This motherfucker is crazy he's never been here since the place has opened, but as soon as this fine ass nigga walk through the door and he's back in Kaniya's office longer than he should be, Lucky wants to show his face.

"Fuck that last I checked I was a silent investor, so I can do what the fuck I want. I'm headed to her office now. I won't say much I know how to act, trust me. I'll be on my best behavior. Don't fucking call her and let her know I'm coming try me and see what the fuck happens," Lucky, Raven, think's she slick trying to cover up for Kaniya.

"Lucky crazy as fuck, I hope Kaniya is conducting business back there." Raven thought to herself.

"I made my way back to Kaniya's office the place actually looks nice filled with black roses. I knocked on the door it was closed." Lucky said. She got me fucked up.

"Come in," Kaniya said. She wasn't expecting anyone.

"What's up Kaniya? Can I holla at you for a minute?" Lucky asked. The fuck she walking around looking all sexy while she's carrying my seeds.

"I'm good Jamel as you can see I have a client. I can't talk right now. I'll get up with you some other time." Kaniya said. I swear this nigga is a stalker, he must have this place bugged.

"I'm finished Mrs. Shannon do you need anything else from me," Dro said. This must be one of her baby daddies.

"I'll wait here until you're finished, let me take you to lunch," Lucky said. Who is this nigga he's not a fucking client he's trying to get with her?

"Mr. Shannon that's all I need from you, and I have a few people that have already registered with the qualifications that you're looking for. I have their resumes, would you like to view them. Would you like for me to set up an interview and how fast do you need them to start?" Kaniya asked. Dro was a slick motherfucker, I know Lucky caught that, he doesn't miss shit.

"No I trust you, they're hired. Check your account I've paid you in full for your services. I'll see you soon neighbor." Dro kissed Kaniya's hand. I know he's mad, that nigga's been grilling me since he walked in the door.

"Kaniya, what the fuck you got going on. You giving your pussy up to your clients now?" Lucky said. Ole boy thinks he slick caught them shots he was throwing he'll catch some slugs too if he wants to play.

"Lucky, why are you here? Why are you worried about who I'm fucking? Last I checked I was a free agent and I have a couple of replacements. You send me black roses every day for what, though. You ain't gon' do shit to me, touch me and get touched. You still fucking with Yirah and God knows who else. Do you see me tripping? Hell no, I'm great like a fresh baked cake?" Kaniya, I'm so tired of his jealous ass. Go on somewhere, would you? Love don't live here anymore.

"Your mouth slick as fuck Kaniya watch what the fuck you say to me.

Pregnancy does a body good. Come here." Lucky said. K want me to put this dick in her life.

"For what, Lucky I don't want you to touching on me and getting free feels. I know you, and I don't want to go there." Kaniya said. Out of all the days, he chose to come here today to show his face.

"I don't want to touch you. If I wanted you Kaniya trust me I could have you, you and I both know it. I want to feel my babies kick. I want them to hear daddies voice, trust me I'm good on your ass too." Lucky said. She didn't like that shit. I don't have to chase her ass no more. I'm straight. I do want to get my dick wet right now, though, but I'm good.

"Well, at least we got that out the way. Go wash your hands first before you touch me. I smell that cheap ass perfume on you. "Kaniya, I can't even trip he's not even my man. I'm not losing any sleep.

"Kaniya, the cheap perfume is bothering you? Damn your titties are full and juicy they look suckable. Why in the fuck are your wearing this tight ass skirt to work and you're pregnant with my seed," Lucky asked. Damn she knows how to piss me off.

"Yeah, my daughter and son don't like to smell cheap shit. They have expensive taste and shit. Hurry up I need to eat my lunch I have another client coming. "I never thought me and Lucky would be in this space where we arguing about everything.

"You see how they kick for daddy? I'm supposed to be doing this shit every day, but you fucked that up. I moved my hand to her breast and start playing with them, one fell out of her bra I used that as my chance to suck on them." I had her right where I wanted her, she didn't stop me she wanted this as much as I did.

"Stop Lucky this is what we are not about to do. I let you feel my stomach because I might be bearing your kids, but my body is off limits. We definitely won't be engaging in any extra activities, that's a fucking no no. Get your ass the fuck up out of my office." Kaniya I can't believe him. Bitch I'm over you, this pussy ain't easy to get you smelling like a bitches' cheap ass perfume, but you want to suck on me. Nah nigga I don't even want no head from you.

"Hey, I tried, I put my hands up so she would know that I'll leave her alone. Let me make some shit clear to you Kaniya, if your babies might not be mine for your sake, you better pray every night them motherfuckers mine because if they ain't I'm bodying you and that fuck nigga on sight. They'll never know their trifling ass momma and bitch ass daddy." I had to get the fuck up out of here before I put my hands on Kaniya. That might not be my babies shit will get her fucking wig split.

"Lucky, make this your last time coming to my place of business do I pop up at your club showing out? I didn't think so.

I'm just being realistic I would love for you to be the father of my kids, but if you're not ain't shit I can do about that, but you can raise the fuck up out of my spot. I'm tired of arguing with you. I invite you to the doctor's appointments, and you never show up, but you want to show up here like you the boss. I'm the fucking boss. As far you killing anybody and my kids not being able know me. Try and die, motherfucker. I got shooters in position that can off your ass too with a blink of an eye. Better yet I'll do it my damn self if you try some fucking bullshit with me when I give birth to my kids. I'm sick of you and all of your threats.

Tell your mammy to keep my name out of her mouth before I introduce her to Kaisha Miller. Whatever feelings you got toward me keep them to yourself because I don't want to disrespect your momma because she's speaking about some half ass shit you telling her. I know you got my spot bugged that's why you showed up because you heard me talking to a man and I peeked his interest. Get your fucking feelings hurt if you want to. That's why I traded my truck in, you had that bitch bugged and a tracker on it. Let me live my life because you are living yours how you see fit." I'm sick of his cockblocking ass.

"Kaniya, your mouth real fucking fly, but keep flirting and shit with clients and I hear you because I do have this motherfucking place bugged. Do anything that's not professional in this fucking office and watch me body your ass. I'll forget really quick that I love you and focus on why I hate you and not give two fucks." Lucky laughed she got me fucked up.

"The door is that way the same way you came in you walk your ass out." Kaniya I've had enough.

"Kaniya, I'm feeling that attitude it's turning me on let me bless you with some dick. I think you need it. You will forever be mine." Lucky laughed as he walked up on her. He was in her face and we were lip to lip, and my hands were around her waist.

"Get your ass the fuck up off of me," Kaniya shouted and shoved Lucky.

"Kaniya, is everything ok?" Raven heard her and Lucky going toe to toe back there about the same shit.

"I'm good, make sure he's gone by the time I get back." Kaniya, I can't deal with Lucky at all.

"I stayed behind a little bit to hear Kaniya and Jamel conversations I was curious. Shawty has mouth on her. I noticed her coming out of the building. Aye Mrs. Shannon, let me take you lunch. The offer still stands, but let me be real with you once you hop in ain't no coming back from this." Dro laughed. I pointed between her and me.

"Kaniya, get your ass in that fucking car and see what happens," Lucky yelled. I knew that nigga wasn't a fucking client. He's trying to fuck. She's hardheaded why would you be trying to kick it with a nigga, and you're pregnant.

"Let's ride." I was more than ready to ride at this point. He peeked my interest. Dro was so fucking sexy he had to be about six foot six and two hundred twenty pounds caramel brown hazel eyes, bottom grill, deep waves, dimples and a beard. I was a bad a girl. This nigga was in a phantom, to top it off he was playing Space Age Pimping by Eight Ball & MJG that was one of my mom's favorites songs. I knew Lucky was hot, bitch. Now play. I'm the fucking boss, bitch.

"What's your story shawty?" Dro asked. Her baby daddy was livid. I knew the nigga from somewhere, though, he knew me too.

"I don't have one I told you everything. Would you like to know any more?" Dro is nosey as hell. He all in my business.

"That was one of your baby daddies?" Dro asked, he still wants you bad ass fuck.

"Yes, he's a potential. Why you heard our conversation? I saw your nosey ass listening." Kaniya laughed.

"I have to know what I'm getting myself into." Dro laughed.

"What are you getting yourself into?" Kaniya said I'm curious to know what Dro was talking about.

"I want to get to know you some more. I'm digging your dab and your mouth is fly as fuck that's another turn on." Dro, I want to see what's up with Kaniya she has a good head on her shoulders.

"Aw, you feeling me already? I think you're fly and handsome as fuck too. How old are you? Do you have any kids, crazy baby mommas? What's your story?" He wanted to know about me I need to about him also.

"Don't flatter yourself shawty? I'm always fly, I was born handsome. I do have one son, I'm thirty, no crazy baby mommas. I don't have a story, I'm a young rich nigga." Dro I wasn't telling her any more than that.

"Where are we going for lunch?" Kaniya, Dro wasn't telling me much he was very discreet.

"Pappadeaux Seafood on Jimmy Carter that's cool with you. Tell me some more about you, though?" Dro thought, shorty fine as hell. I met her at the wrong time, though. We could be friends though if it goes further than that it is what is.

For My Savage, I Will Ride or Die

BCPL
Baltimore County
Public Library

CPSIA information can be obtained
at www.ICGtesting.com
Printed in the USA
LVOW10s2122100417

530296LV00015B/650/P